Odd Awakenings

Short Southern Fiction

Stephanie Arban Holt

Harpe's Head Literary

Odd Awakenings:
Short Southern Fiction

Cover Art by Margaret Harden Brown
Cover Design by Tabitha Short

ISBN-10: 978-0692643471
ISBN-13: 0692643478

First Edition Published by
Harpe's Head Literary
Hanson, Kentucky

Printed in the United States of America

CONTENTS

Ryman

Ryman was a willowy young man with a curious perpetual twinkle in his eyes. Most enjoyed his company, but found him rather odd. Not because of the perpetual twinkle or his unwavering good nature, for no one could remember ever seeing him unhappy, not even his parents, Wilma and Joe. No, it was because of his "gift," as Wilma called it. Ryman, you see, had visions—visions that foretold the future. And to date, all of his visions that could not be avoided, and of course those that people refused to try to avoid, had come to pass.

One would think that such a gift would be quite advantageous, a winning lotto ticket to good health, wealth and happiness. For Ryman, this was unfortunately not the case. The problem was that his visions were, for the most part, about the mundane—such as a cow dying, a well running dry, the mayor losing his car keys, or the coming of locusts in other parts of the world. And because of this, some scoffed at his prophecies. Others, however, had come to believe in him, especially after the summer when he predicted that Jenny Stewart, who was very pregnant at the time, would deliver twin boys. She did just that three days later.

Jenny, who had gone all through school with Ryman and had seen his visions come to pass many times, prudently exchanged the single stroller she'd purchased at J.C. Penny's for a double one the day before she delivered. Her husband, a burly and disagreeable deputy sheriff who hailed from Memphis, had thought she was mad.

When Jenny told him about Ryman's vision, he told her she was being foolish, adding that, "There are no twins on either side of our families, and the doc would have told us if you had two buns in the oven, don'tcha think?" After his twins were born, Deputy Dan took to avoiding Ryman whenever possible, just as one avoids walking under a ladder, even though they profess to not be superstitious.

That had been nearly ten years ago, and Ryman would be turning thirty this coming July 4th. Joe always joked, "Ryman's good nature is due to the fact that he was born on a holiday made for beer drinkin', back yard barbecuin', and celebratin' freedom!"

Joe himself was an expert on all three. His wife, on the other hand, hated the taste and smell of beer, and she couldn't grill a steak, or a hamburger for that matter, if her life depended on it. And from the time she said "I do" some thirty-five years prior, at the budding age of seventeen, Wilma had known very little of freedom in her life.

On this particular Friday afternoon, as Wilma folded a load of laundry and Joe worked on sharpening the blades on his lawnmower before putting it away for the season, Ryman, who had never married or left home, put on his Atlanta Braves sweatshirt and headed down the sidewalk to the corner IGA store. It was late fall in West Virginia, and he breathed in the crisp, cool air as he walked, finding the smell of decaying leaves to be a pleasant one.

Once he'd passed the widow Mills' house, he crossed the street and walked down the sidewalk on that side for two blocks, and then crossed back. He heard Mr. Thornton's shepherd barking a block back and smiled. Two days ago, he'd had a vision of the unruly dog, which Thornton had un-creatively named Rover, lunging for him and breaking his chain.

"River's gonna rise," Ryman boldly announced to Billy Wiley, the owner of the independent grocery, as he came through the IGA's new automatic door. There was a whoosh as the door closed behind him.

"You don't say?" Billy responded, raising his bushy eyebrows and winking at Mrs. Larson as he bagged up her apples and bananas.

"Yessir. Several feet, I'd say."

"Several feet? Well, I'll declare, son. If it rises that much, it's liable to wash our little 'ol town of River Bend right off the damn map!" Billy exclaimed, and then laughed so hard he got what the old timers called a "coughing fit."

Bill Wiley had smoked two packs of Camels a day since he was twelve. He'd always been overweight, and he hadn't worked a single day at hard labor his entire life. Now, at fifty-six, Billy's remaining days on this earth were but few.

"Besides, it's punkin' season, son, not springtime," he added between laughter and coughs as he handed Mrs. Larson her change.

"You see that in one of your visions, Ryman?" Edgar Jones asked, almost in a whisper as he got up off of the edge of the cooler he was sitting on and walked over to Ryman, ignoring Billy's comment and coughing fit.

"Yessir. Several feet," Ryman repeated, nodding his head this time as though satisfied with his estimate.

"Can ya tell when the rain's comin'? About how long would you say we've got before it starts?"

"Not gonna rain," Ryman said slowly, a little puzzled by this proclamation himself.

Edgar stood in front of him and blinked a few times. Billy started laugh-coughing again so hard that his face started to turn blue. Mrs. Larson grabbed her grocery sack and nearly ran to the new automatic door after a projectile of phlegm exited Billy's mouth and landed on the checkout counter about an inch from her faux leather pocketbook.

"Not gonna rain," Edgar said slowly, not as a question, but as a theory to be contemplated or an option to be weighed.

"Nosir."

"So...where do ya suppose the water's gonna come from?" Edgar asked.

"Dunno."

"Dam up in Morgantown could break, I suppose, but seems that would cause The Snake to rise a heap more than several feet."

The Okachoke River, which skirted River Bend on three sides, had been called "The Snake" by the locals for years, although its Chickasaw Indian name actually meant wild pig.

"Dunno," Ryman repeated, and then shrugged and headed for the snack isle.

Although he had succeeded without effort to maintain a slim build all his life, Ryman was a junk food junkie. He hated most vegetables and rarely ate meat. His diet routinely consisted of sweets, fruits, cornbread, pasta, pizza, and gallons of buttermilk. Wilma was constantly nagging him about it. "You're not sixteen anymore, Ryman," she would say. "One of these days you're gonna either get really fat or have a heart attack, or both!" Ryman paid little attention.

After paying for his family size bag of peanut M&Ms, unfazed by Billy's continued ribbing about his vision, Ryman left the IGA and headed to Mayor Jackson's office downtown. He thought it was the least he could do.

"Well good afternoon, Ryman," Sandy Adkins, who was Jenny Stewart's younger sister and the mayor's new assistant, said when he walked in.

"River's gonna rise," Ryman announced, forgoing pleasantries as usual. "Several feet. Folks need to leave now," he added.

Although Sandy had known Ryman for several years and had become accustomed to his odd nature, her immediate response was much the same as Edgar's. Her smile faded and she opened her mouth to speak, but didn't utter a word. She sat gaping at him, blinking, trying to think of what to say. It was not an attractive look for the former homecoming queen.

"Would you tell the mayor? And tell Jenny too," Ryman added, and then turned and left the mayor's office.

Next, he headed to the post office, library, and beauty salon—in that order. At each stop, he heralded his breaking news, knowing that those present at these strategic locations would spread the word to the whole town by sundown. Still, for good measure, he stopped by the elementary school on his way home to inform Principal Moss.

"Kids should get on the busses and head out of town," he told Moss. "The Snake's gonna rise. Don't know when it's gonna rise, but soon maybe," he added.

The principal, like Edgar and Sandy, was at a loss for words at first, but recovered quickly and assured Ryman that the children would be safe. In truth, he had no intention of ending the last class of the day early and bussing all of the kids out of town. Even if he did believe in Ryman's visions, which he didn't, calling all of their parents would take hours, and it was his poker night.

By the time Ryman got back home, he'd eaten the entire bag of M&Ms he'd purchased at the IGA except for one handful. And as he walked up the driveway, his last handful of M&Ms part way to his mouth, he had another vision, this one a series of snapshots in time.

He stood motionless, eyes wide open and staring into the back yard at nothing. But what he saw was a vivid image. Not of the back yard, but of himself sitting on top of a chimney and worrying about getting soot on the seat of his new jeans. Then, he saw his mother drowning. Next, his father was on fire. Finally, Rover was licking the back of Mr. Thornton's head as his owner lay face down and half submerged in thick, brown mud.

Ryman tossed the last handful of treats in his mouth and licked the palm of his right hand. He thought how the commercials were wrong. M&Ms

will melt in your hand if you leave them there long enough.

He then walked on up the driveway and into the side door of his house. His father was napping and snoring on the sofa in the living room. His mother was frying chicken in the kitchen. He walked up behind her and hugged her tightly as he squeezed his eyes shut, trying to get the image of her drowning out of his mind. She smiled and asked him where he'd been.

"Gotta go *now*, Mom," he said. "River's gonna rise. Soon. You'll drown. Gotta go. *Now.*"

Wilma's right hand froze, the half-browned chicken leg stuck in mid-flip at the end of the fork, suspended above the sizzling grease in the frying pan. Ryman didn't wait for her reply. He moved into the living room, sat down on the coffee table in front of the sofa, and began to gently shake his sleeping father's shoulder. Joe was slow to wake, since most of the six-pack he'd downed while working on the lawnmower was still making its rounds through his system.

"Wake up, Dad. Gotta go. The Snake's gonna rise. Gotta go *now!*"

"What?" Joe mumbled, opened his eyes, and stared at his son. "What's the matter with you, boy?"

"River's gonna rise," Ryman repeated, smiling down at his father.

"I reckon," Joe said, rolling over to face the back of the sofa.

"*Now*, Dad. Gotta go."

"Hum?" was all his father could manage.

Within seconds after Ryman left the kitchen to go wake his father, Wilma had turned off the burner, washed her hands, ran to the bedroom, drug the large suitcase out of the closet, and began throwing clothes into it. She ran upstairs to Ryman's room and grabbed some underwear and socks out of his dresser drawers, and then a few shirts and pants out of his closet. She ran back downstairs, threw those pieces into the bulging suitcase and sat on it to zip it closed. Next, she pulled the fireproof box from beneath the bed, grabbed her purse by the nightstand, and ran with them out the side door to the garage. She started their green '57 Buick sedan, backed it out of the garage and about half way down the drive to the side door of the house, put it in park, and ran back inside.

"Get the suitcase out of my bedroom and put it in the trunk of the car, Ryman," she yelled as she plucked her wedding photo and Ryman's baby picture off of the mantle above the fireplace, and then grabbed the blue and yellow afghan her grandmother had crocheted off the back of the rocking chair.

"Gotta go," Ryman said as he calmly stood and walked to his parent's bedroom to fetch the suitcase as he was told, leaving his father to continue snoring peacefully on the sofa.

After rounding up a few more essential items, including a grocery bag filled with canned food and a stash of cash she'd hidden in an empty flour sack in the back of the pantry, Wilma raced back out to the car and threw them all in the back seat.

"Get in the back, Ryman," she instructed, and then ran back into the house and into the kitchen, where she grabbed a pot from the pot rack and a large serving spoon from the drawer beside the sink. "Joseph!" she yelled, banging the spoon on the pan as she flew into the living room. "Get up! Get up! The house is on fire!"

"What?" Joe said, but the metallic racket and his wife's shrill screams calling for help successfully roused him. He sat up on the edge of the sofa and stared at her. "What the hell's wrong with you?" he asked.

"Get in the car. I've collected everything. Do it. Don't ask why. It's an emergency and you're half asleep. I'll drive. Go! Now!"

Mumbling obscenities, Joe walked outside and got into the passenger's seat of the car, still too sleepy and tipsy to argue. Wilma locked up and was behind the wheel seconds later.

"Where do we go?" she asked Ryman, looking at him in the rearview mirror as she started backing the car down the driveway.

"Dunno," he said, smiling.

"Edna's...we'll go to your aunt Edna's. She's twenty miles north, and she lives on a ridge. That oughta be high enough, right?"

"Um...yes, I think so," Ryman said slowly, and then nodded quickly and looked out the window, still smiling.

Wilma took that as a good sign and headed north. She rolled her window down half way so the cool breeze would hit her face. Now that they were away, the panic was starting to set in. She kept going over all of the people in River Bend she needed to call and warn when they reached her sister's house.

The next morning, Ryman and his family sat in his Aunt Edna's living room watching the news on her black & white RCA television. The weatherman was giving a frost warning for the region, but the camera switched back to the news anchor before the weatherman got to the extended weekly forecast.

"We're interrupting our local weather report momentarily for a breaking news story," the handsome newsman announced excitedly as he pushed his black, horn-rimmed glasses further up on his nose. They rarely got "breaking news" in his small West Virginia city, and he was anxious for the opportunity to deliver it. "Just moments ago, tragedy struck at the Dalton Mine in River Bend. The miners, who were working in a shaft that runs parallel with the side of the mountain, blasted a seam of coal that was close to the surface. The blast blew a hole in the side of the mountain just above the Okachoke River. Initial reports state that no miners were hurt in the explosion. However, the explosion sent rock, soil and trees raining down into the Okachoke at one of its narrowest spans, creating a makeshift dam." The newsman paused for a second or two and stared at the camera for effect, then continued more slowly, emphasizing each word. "Residents of River Bend are strongly urged to leave the area *at once.*"

Ryman's family looked at him with expressions of awe on their faces, and then looked from one to the other, and then back at Ryman, who didn't notice. He was sitting close to the TV, smiling as usual, watching and listening to the newsman intently.

"The river will continue to rise," the newsman was saying, "and will likely cause catastrophic flooding along its banks. News 27 is attempting to contact the mayor of River Bend at this time. It is still unknown as to whether evacuation procedures have begun, but residents closest to the river are advised to leave their homes and seek shelter on higher ground."

As the newsman began to repeat his breaking news story, Edna got up from her arm chair and turned the television off. "Well my heavens, I'm so thankful that you all came up here last night, Wilma," she said, and then turned to Ryman and asked, "Is that what you saw in your vision, hun? Was it the side of the mountain coming down in the river?"

"No ma'am. Didn't see that part. Just the river rising."

"Well my heavens," she repeated, her hand covering her mouth. After a moment, she added, "Who's hungry? Might as well eat us some breakfast. We've called everyone we know. Nothin' more to do but wait and see what happens."

Wilma agreed and went with her sister to the kitchen to make some biscuits. Joe got up and turned the television back on, but switched channels and found a movie he and Wilma had gone to see in the theater a few years before: *Bedtime for Bonzo.*

He sat back down beside Ryman and got comfortable, wishing Wilma had thought to grab some beer when she was gathering up supplies. Later, after he'd had his breakfast, he would see if he could find a store in the neighborhood that sold Pabst.

"Hey," Ryman said casually, "that fella right there is going to be the president one day."

Joe started to laugh, but then stopped abruptly and stared at Ronald Reagan playing Professor Peter Boyd in *Bedtime for Bonzo* on the small screen.

The Heirloom

Joseph Alexander was an only child and the sole heir of the beautiful two-story antebellum home he had grown up in. It was centered on a large lot on the north side of a quiet, downtown side street, which was lined with mature cypress, birch, and pine trees. His parents, Robert and Beatrice, had purchased the estate from Beatrice's parents and had lived there for nearly sixty years.

Robert, who had worked tirelessly on the old home throughout the years to keep it in pristine condition, had died the previous winter of a heart attack while chopping wood for the fireplace. In early spring, his beloved wife followed him in death, passing away peacefully in her sleep with her head upon her husband's pillow. The old Southern estate now belonged to Joseph, and he and his wife had begun minor renovations to make it their own. One day, they would pass it on to their daughter, Amelia.

After lunch one Saturday afternoon that summer, sixteen year-old Amelia B. Alexander was sitting on the white front porch swing, taking a break from her chores. She had been working most of the morning on arranging her bedroom closet while her parents painted the newly remodeled kitchen a bright buttery yellow. It was a hot, sunny day, and before long, Amelia was napping, her head resting on colorful new pillows that her mother had just purchased for the porch swing.

She dreamt of her grandparents, of the way her grandfather's thick beard always tickled her, and how he always smelled like Old Spice. She dreamt of her grandmother's wonderfully delicious biscuits topped with butter and honey. She then saw herself playing in the yard and her grandmother calling to her from the front door. When she looked up, she saw a young woman in the doorway, her grandmother from an era before Amelia's time, an image she had only seen in family photographs. To the right, she saw a handsome, middle-aged man watching from the kitchen window with a smile on his face. She then heard her grandfather's booming, jolly voice as he sang some silly song while stoking the fire in the parlor on the other side of the house. She ran up the front porch steps in her dream and could vividly feel her grandmother's warm hug as she entered the cozy home.

When Amelia awoke, she stretched and ran her slender fingers through the thick, auburn hair she'd inherited from her father, pulling it back into a ponytail, holding it away from her face. It was now damp with summer sweat.

She recalled her dream and felt comforted to be living in her grandparent's home. Although she had hated leaving her friends and her school back in St. Louis, she didn't miss the crowded city. She was excited that her parents allowed her to drive much more often now that they lived in a smaller town. She'd soon be turning seventeen and was looking forward to her last year of high school before attending college, to making a whole new set of friends, and to embarking on new adventures.

Looking out over the front lawn, Amelia's gaze was drawn to the bright red roses on either side of the lattice arbor, marking the entry to the winding stone path that led to the front porch steps. Robert had built the arbor for Beatrice the day Joseph was born, a joyous and unexpected event later in life. The roses were another gift given to her on that day by a dear friend, clipped from his own heirloom rose bush. They were as beautiful as Amelia's grandmother had been—robust, full of vibrant color, unpruned.

When she pulled her hands from her hair, Amelia felt something on the first finger of her right hand. She stared at it, wondering where it had come from. The ring was not hers. She'd never seen it before. Pulling it off and looking at it closely, she noticed that it looked like a man's wedding band, silver and worn.

"Good morning, Miss Amelia."

Startled, she looked up quickly and saw the old man in faded jeans and a short sleeved, checked shirt standing on the lawn, leaning on the handle of his rake.

"Oh! Hello, Mr. Flannigan."

"That's Uncle Flannigan to you, missy," he said with a slight Irish accent and a warning wag of his first finger. "Your dad's been calling me 'Uncle' all his life. 'Bout time you did too. Mr. Flannigan was my dear old father's name, rest his soul."

She smiled. "But you're not really his uncle, are you?"

"Well no...not really, but all the same," he said with a sentimental smile. "Whatcha got there?" he added after a moment.

Amelia looked down at the ring. "Um, well, it's the strangest thing. It's a silver ring. I was taking a nap on the swing, and when I woke up, it was on my finger. But I swear it isn't mine, and I didn't put it on my finger. Actually, it looks like a man's ring. It's pretty big, way too big for my finger, and kind of wide, you know," she said, staring at it once more.

"You don't say," Mr. Flannigan remarked, moving a little closer to the front porch. "You know, you look very much like your grandmother did when she was young, about your age."

"That's what everybody says," Amelia replied, her attention still on the mysterious ring that had suddenly appeared on her finger.

"Well, maybe a little sprite, or your fairy godfather left that pretty little ring there for you," he said.

She looked up and gave him a disbelieving look. He gave her a little wink in return.

"Sure, I'll bet that's exactly what happened," she said, rolling her eyes. "And besides, I think girls have fairy *godmothers*, not godfathers."

"Who says?" he asked, feigning indignation. They both laughed.

Amelia studied the ring once more, trying it on different fingers. "You know, this sort of looks like the ring my grandmother wore, not her wedding ring, but one she wore on her other hand. There's a design of a vine with leaves all around it, just like she had on hers. This one is way too big to be hers, though. Maybe it was my grandfather's. I'll have to ask Dad. It's just so weird how it just appeared on my finger!"

Mr. Flannigan turned to look at the rose bushes beside the arbor as Amelia was talking. "We all grew up together—me, Robert, and your grandmother," he said solemnly. "We were the best of friends. Went to school together, played together, and lived right here next door to each other for many years, our whole lives really. We sure had some fun times, we did. I miss those days, and I miss my old friends. There wasn't anything we wouldn't do for each other, you know."

"So, you were their neighbor when my dad was little?"

"Oh sure. Was right there the day he was born."

Amelia watched the old man as he stood on the stone path in the front yard, looking out at the arbor and roses. He seemed sad and lonely to her, and she thought he'd probably stopped by just wanting to chat. She wondered what all he had seen and done in his lifetime, what the world was like when he was young.

"Are you married, Mr... *Uncle* Flannigan?" she asked.

He turned back to her, wiped at his eyes with the back of his hand and chuckled. "No, no, never married. Been a bachelor all these years."

"What kind of work did you do, if you don't mind my asking?"

"I was a gardener, Miss Amelia," he said as he turned back toward the porch and leaned on the stair rail. "Still am, I suppose." He held up his rake as evidence. "Only now, I just garden for myself. I'll bet there isn't a flower garden in the neighborhood I haven't been hired to tend at one time or another over the years, though."

"Well, I'll bet you were a fine gardener," she said, and then looked over at his front yard and noticed for the first time all of the beautiful flowers in various garden plots, the manicured bushes, and the expertly trimmed ornamental trees. "Oh, your yard is really beautiful. I really hadn't noticed before. It's the prettiest on the whole block by far!"

"Why, I do think you're right, if I say so myself," he said, smiling broadly.

"And you have some of grandmother's rose bushes!" she noticed, pointing. "Yours are huge!"

"I do indeed. Hers grew from a clipping off of mine. Planted them for her myself the very day your father was born."

"Oh, I remember that story. Gran told me. She loved the trellis arbor and those rose bushes. She always made Grandpa give the arbor a fresh coat of paint each year, and I remember helping her trim the rose bushes when I'd come to visit each summer. We'd always snip off enough to make a lovely bouquet to sit on the coffee table, and she'd let me arrange the bouquet myself."

He laughed and nodded, remembering how his friend had always lovingly tended the rose bushes. He then looked up at Amelia and said softly, "Beatrice didn't think she could have a child, you know. She and Robert tried for several years, but no luck." He looked back out at the bushes once more.

"Really? I never knew that."

Joe Flannigan nodded, and then turned and gave Amelia a little wave. "Well, I'd best be going. I've tended my garden. Now it's my turn for a nap." He chuckled, and then turned back for a moment, leaning on the handle of his rake once more. "You take good care of that pretty ring now, Miss Amelia. It looks like a fine old heirloom."

The Escalator

Ramona Martina caressed each of the pale pink cashmere sweaters as she gently folded them and placed them on the shelf. She loved the soft, silky feel of the fabric. Her stomach growled beneath her own simple, white cotton blouse and she looked at the Timex she'd worn since high school. *Fifteen minutes until lunchtime*, she thought, wishing she had packed the apple she'd splurged on at the grocery yesterday instead of saving it for an evening snack.

After returning a rack to the dressing room, Ramona looked over at the escalator, hoping to see Angie Lofton descending. The two young women didn't socialize outside of work much, but considered each other best friends anyway, ever since they had started working at Claymore's department store on the same day ten years earlier. Their friendship surprised fellow co-workers; the two women were nothing alike.

Twenty-eight year-old Ramona was from south Ellisville, Louisiana. Her father was a mechanic who often worked as a handyman on the side. Her mother had never been employed, but she excelled at providing her husband and their brood of four children with nourishing meals and a warm, safe home filled with love. The family lived in a small, three bedroom, brick ranch built in the 1950s, which was in need of repair and cosmetic updates.

Ramona had secured full-time employment the very day she graduated from high school and moved out on her own the year her youngest brother was born. Her small, one bedroom apartment was on the third floor of a large complex, but it was the first time she'd ever had a bedroom to herself, and she loved it. Although the space was compact, she always kept it clean and tidy. And she had furnished and decorated it nicely with thrift store items and refinished garage sale finds.

Since she was single, Ramona usually offered to work weekends and holidays so that her co-workers with children could spend more time with their loved ones. She worked hard, opting for as much overtime as she could get, and was generous with gift-giving during Christmas and birthdays. It was her way of helping her parents out financially.

But being a rather shy loner and work-a-holic resulted in few opportunities for forming romantic relationships. In fact, she'd had only two boyfriends her entire life, and one of those was in high school. She had potential, though, as her mother was always quick to point out. She was thin, pretty, graceful, and well-mannered—everything that successful men seemed to want in women, in a wife. So, Ramona felt that there was still hope, despite the other fact that her mother was quick to point out: she was no longer a "spring chicken."

Her friend Angie was thirty and from the north side of Ellisville, where she still lived with her parents. She always told everyone that she wasn't actually living with them, but rather renting the guest house beside their in-ground pool. Only Ramona knew that, according to Angie, she kept offering to pay rent, but her parents had kept refusing to accept it. Early on in their friendship, Ramona suspected that this was why Angie was able to afford her shiny new Cadillac, which was fire engine red, of course. Everything about Angie was fire engine red.

Her equally charismatic father, Thomas Lofton, owned two car dealerships and could be seen most every evening on TV, pitching his SUVs, trucks and sedans. Her mother, Helen, was a member of the Garden Club and chair of the local Red Hat Society. Angie's only sibling, blond and blue-eyed

Thomas Hale Lofton III, was a budding golf pro at the Ellisville Country Club.

Angie was tall and buxom, with curves in all the right places, which she expertly accentuated with her extensive high-fashion wardrobe. Her shoulder length, golden blonde hair was always coiffured and her nails always painted, usually bright red. And one thing Ramona noticed early on was that Angie apparently owned a multitude of earrings; she couldn't recall ever seeing her wear the same pair more than twice.

At exactly noon on this particular day, Ramona's replacement showed up from the shoe department to cover her station. She logged off the cash register and started toward the break room. As she passed the escalator, she looked up once more, wondering what was keeping Angie, who often found an excuse to sneak away a few minutes early for lunch. Sometimes she'd tell her replacement that she just couldn't wait to go to the restroom, or that she had an important call to make.

Once in the break room, Ramona grabbed her insulated sack from her locker, switched on the small TV mounted near the ceiling in the corner of the room, and changed the station to her favorite soap opera. She secretly had a crush on the ruggedly handsome lead actor, Vincent O'Neal.

Anxious to watch the new episode, Ramona quickly filled her drink bottle from the water cooler and found a seat facing the television. She was sure that Vincent's character would recover from the gunshot wound he had sustained in the last episode, the result of a botched attempted hit that his ex-lover had put out on him. As Ramona was unwrapping her sandwich, Angie burst through the break room door, giggling girlishly.

"What's up, girlfriend?" Angie asked as she headed to the refrigerator.

"Not much, just watching my soap."

"How can you watch that awful show? The acting is so lame." Angie retrieved her lunch, bought a soda from the machine, and sat across from Ramona, her back to the TV. She opened the take-out container and started shoveling forkfuls of La Bistro's signature chef salad between her bright red lips. "I woke up craving this salad this morning, so I called Mommy and she brought one over for me on her way to her garden club meeting. She's the best!"

Ramona smiled and nodded, but didn't take her eyes from the screen.

"Guess what!"

"What?"

"Our new Assistant Store Manager, Greg Smith, couldn't keep his eyes off of me at the staff meeting yesterday. Did you notice? You were sitting right next to me. Did you see him? It was *soooo* obvious," she said. "Bologna and mustard sandwich again?" Angie added, wrinkling her nose at what her friend was eating.

"He's really not that new. He's been here nearly a year now," Ramona said. "What did he say to you?" she asked absently, trying to listen to her show over Angie's rather high-pitched chatter.

"Nothing! That's my point. He just kept staring. Every time I looked up from filing my nails, he was staring at me, and when our eyes met, he smiled and looked away. He did it quickly, ya know, like he was embarrassed. Wow! Wouldn't that be something, me dating the Store Manager?"

"*Assistant* Store Manager," Ramona corrected with a smile.

"Still, he'll probably be the manager one day, and I know he makes good money. Tammy in Accounting said all managers make nearly six figures. That'll do just fine, ya know. I'm not looking for a millionaire. Wouldn't find one in this town anyway. I just want a guy that makes a good living so I can quit this crummy job."

"And live in a nice house," Ramona said, nodding but still watching the soap opera.

"Exactly!"

"And buy nice clothes and shoes, and earrings of course, without worrying about pinching pennies."

"Oh sure. Lots of new things...especially earrings!" Angie agreed.

"And have 2.5 kids."

"Ewww, no. No kids. I'm not good with little kids. And besides, they ruin your body, ya know."

31

Ramona shook her head and chuckled. "So what's your next move?"

"Oh, I've got it all figured out!"

Ramona nodded, finished her sandwich, opened her small bag of chips, and went to refill her water bottle. "And?" she coaxed, knowing that her friend was dying to tell her all the details of her plan to "hook Mr. Right," which this week was apparently Mr. Smith.

"Well, when it gets close to 5:00, I'm going down the hall to Human Resources. I'll ask how many vacation days I have left or something. I know I have over a week left, but they don't know I know that. So anyway, his office is right next door. On my way out, I'll pop in and ask if I can have next Friday off. I could take it off anyway to go to my cousin's wedding, but it's not like it's a big deal if I don't go, if Greg says no, I mean. Anyway, so then I'll just casually mention that I'm going down to Ramsey's for a drink with some friends after work and ask him if he'd like to join us. So...you've got to come have a drink with me tonight.

Ramona stopped watching the TV, looked her friend in the eye for the first time during lunch, and started shaking her head. "Sorry, I've got to stop by the grocery store and then do some laundry. I'm down to my last pair of underwear."

"Oh girl, you've always got chores. How do you ever expect to find a man when all you do is work and then run back home every night? Come on! It's Friday, and it's payday. Live a little!"

Ramona closed her eyes, sighed, and agreed to meet Angie for a drink, just one drink, if she promised to be quiet for the rest of their lunch break so she could see the end of her soap opera. Angie smiled, nodded, and remained silent for the next ten minutes.

At 2:00 that afternoon, Ramona was surprised when she looked up after helping a customer and saw Angie coming down the escalator. She was in tears and looked awful. Ramona quickly keyed in her code to lock the register and rushed over to her as she stepped onto the first floor. She asked what was wrong, but Angie wouldn't stop long enough to tell her. She headed for the front doors of the department store, nearly running.

Ramona kept pace with her and kept asking what had happened. Terrible things ran through her mind. Maybe a family member had been in an accident. Finally, when they reached the doors, Angie stopped and turned to Ramona.

"I was fired!" she spat.

"What?" Ramona was shocked.

"Yep, fired. After ten years. No warning." Angie pushed on through the door and Ramona followed her out to the sidewalk.

"Well...well, what did they say? Didn't they give you a reason?"

"Not really, just that they're 'making some personnel changes,'" she said, bursting into tears again. She fumbled in her purse for a second and pulled out a white envelope. "They gave me a check for two week's severance pay," she added, holding up the envelope as proof.

With that, Angie stuffed the envelope back in her purse and ran out to her shiny red Cadillac. She jumped in and sped out of the parking lot without a glance back. Ramona stood outside Claymore's and stared after her, still in shock, wishing she had given Angie a hug or at least said goodbye.

When she returned to her station, Ramona found two customers waiting. She apologized, quickly unlocked her register, and went back to work. She stayed busy for the next couple of hours, but her anxiety grew. She wondered if she would be next on the company's chopping block and was mentally making plans for what she would do if that were the case.

At 4:15, the phone beside her register rang. It was Barbara Clayton in Human Resources saying that said she was sending another sales clerk over to finish out Ramona's shift. She was to report to Mr. Smith immediately.

Ramona's heart began to race and her hand trembled as she hung up the phone. She felt sick. Many things crossed her mind as she saw the other clerk approach. She wondered why this was happening. She truly felt that she had been a good employee, so she wondered if the department store was in financial trouble or something, and if there was any way she could save her job.

Collecting herself and refusing to panic, she smiled and thanked the other clerk for covering for her. As she made her way to the escalator, she promised herself that she wouldn't cry as Angie had. She'd been very frugal and had ample savings built up, enough to last her for months if necessary. She would just tighten her belt a bit more, ask Mr. Smith for a good recommendation, and go out on Monday morning to search for another job.

When Ramona ascended to the next level, she stepped off of the escalator and made her way to the Assistant Manager's office, trying to stand tall and confident. Mr. Smith was standing in the doorway waiting for her, a welcoming smile on his face.

"Ms. Martina, thank you for coming up. Come in and have a seat," he said.

Ramona smiled back, but was too tense to respond. She perched on the edge of the chair beside his desk, crossed her legs at the ankles, and tried to prepare herself for the worst.

"Ms. Martina, you have done an outstanding job here at Claymore's. You started as a clerk and were then promoted to Lead Associate. You've done well in that position also and have trained and managed over twenty Claymore employees over the past few years. Additionally, you have streamlined several procedures, helping to make this one of the company's most efficient stores. We'd like to reward you for that service and your dedication to this company, Ms. Martina. I've called you here today to offer you another promotion, quite a nice one, actually."

Ramona exhaled. "A...a promotion?" was all she could manage. She relaxed her grip on the armchair.

"Yes. Mr. Higgins will be retiring next month, and he has offered me his position as Store Manager. I've accepted. This will leave my position vacant. I'd like you to fill that vacancy, Ramona." He paused, but she just stared at him in disbelief, unable to speak. "It would require that you attend a two week training program, purchase a few nice business suits, and switch from hourly to salary. You would have this office and I'll move into Mr. Higgins', and we would give you a small allowance to redecorate. I realize it's a bit manly now and hasn't been spruced up in several years." Ramona looked around, smiled, and nodded. "You'll be expected to come in a little earlier each day, but will have weekends and holidays off. Your paid vacation time will also increase to five weeks per year. Finally, I have been authorized to double your current salary." He paused again, but Ramona still did not speak, so he went on. "I'd like your answer by tomorrow if possible. We're working on a bit of a tight timeline. We'll be making several personnel changes and will do some hiring to cover floor positions, which you would be heavily involved in if you accept the position."

After a moment, Ramona blurted out, "Yes!"

Greg Smith laughed. "Excellent."

"Thank you so much," Ramona said, collecting herself. "I sincerely appreciate this opportunity, Mr. Smith, and I look forward to serving Claymore's as the new Assistant Manager...and to working with you closely on day-to-day operations. I have a few ideas on how we might expedite the hiring and training process that I'd like to share with you, when we have time. There is, however, just one request that I have."

"Fantastic!" he said, looking genuinely pleased. "I'm so glad you've accepted the job offer, Ramona. What is your request?"

"That you call me Mona."

Greg Smith leaned back in his executive chair and laughed heartily. "No problem. I like Mona much better, too. And I'd love to hear those ideas you have, the sooner the better."

She smiled and thought for a moment. "Well, I'm supposed to meet a friend at Ramsey's for a drink after work. Would you like to join us?" she asked, knowing that Angie wouldn't be there. "It will give me a chance to offer my suggestions and to ask a few questions about administrative protocol."

"I'd love to join you for a drink," he said, returning her smile. "Great idea. I'll meet you there in say...an hour?"

"Perfect. Perhaps a nice glass of wine will make my plan more attractive."

He looked up at her and smiled. "I'm sure no wine is needed, but we'll toast to your promotion and I'll answer any questions you have."

"See you in a bit then," she said.

Mona stood, shook Greg's hand, and went to collect her things from the hourly break room for the last time. The day had been quite an emotional rollercoaster. Now, she was ecstatic and making all new plans.

As she retrieved her insulated lunch bag and water bottle from the locker, she wondered if Angie would be selling her red Cadillac.

A Murder Mystery

"I don't see why we had to drive all night in this downpour just to be there in time for breakfast, Adam. Your insistence annoys me."

"Lily, I told you. The whole event starts at breakfast this morning. That's when they group us up into teams. Breakfast is at 8:00 and it's already 7:30. Do you think we'll make it on time?"

"Yes! Geeze, don't have a stroke. We're almost there according to the GPS. If you gave me the right address to enter, that is."

"I'm just really excited. I've been wanting to go to one of these for years. Please don't spoil it for me. You're always so...so discontented.

"Really? Ya think?"

"You agreed to come with me, so why not try to have a good time. It'll be a good opportunity for you to just rest and relax...de-stress. Being out in nature is the best way to do that."

"De-stress? This crap just stresses me out more. I'm still betting that it's going to be a boring weekend with a bunch of bookish nerds. This is just not my thing, Adam. But yes, I did agree, reluctantly, to come along after you refused to shut up about it. They just better have a big, modern TV in our room at this state park, and a pool would be really nice, *and* Wi-Fi. I'll have to have something to entertain myself while you run around with your little group playing make-believe detectives. You *did* bring the laptop, right?"

"Yes, it's in the back seat. Wouldn't you enjoy trying to solve the mystery? Come on. It'll be a hoot!"

"Depends on who's getting murdered. Maybe I'll get lucky and it'll be *you!* Good thing I've made sure your life insurance is paid up, huh?"

"There it is! Up on that ridge. Wow, cool place. Slow down a little, will ya. The turn must be just up ahead."

"You can be so childish. I see the turn. If I'd wanted children, we would have had a boat load. And don't embarrass me like you did at that stupid science fiction convention you drug me to last year. You're thirty-four, not fourteen."

"I would have loved to have kids. Kids are great. You know, you're not too old yet. Sure you don't want to reconsider? Lots of women are waiting until their thirties...even their forties.

And you're so thin and beautiful. I don't know why you're worried that it'll make you 'fat and ugly.'"

"We've been married, what, something like forever, and you still don't get me, do you, Adam? I should never have married you in the first place. We have absolutely nothing in common."

"I think it's safe to say I do understand you, Lilith. Look, there's a spot close to the door. Let's go on in since we're running late. I'll come back and get our bags after breakfast. Okay?"

"Fine."

"Wow! This place is awesome. You really feel like you're out in the middle of nowhere, totally immersed in nature. And what a beautiful lake. It has a healing effect. Instantly calming, don't you think?"

"You are so weird. I'm so sick of your hippy-dippy, love and peace and harmony crap. What? What's that sad, puppy dog look for?"

"Nothing.

"Are you crying? Really?"

"Let it go, Lily."

"Maybe I will one day, Adam, when you grow a pair."

"There's the registration desk over there."

"Yeah, I see it. I'll take care of checking us in."

"Hello! I'm Gabe. Welcome to Kentucky's finest national park. Do you have a reservation?"

"Of course. The reservation is listed under my husband's name, Adam Newman."

"Oh! Mr. Newman. Yes, yes, of course. We'll take care of you right away!"

"Well geeze, he's not a movie star or anything. We're supposed to be booked for a cabin by the lake. Two occupants for two *glorious* nights, I'm sure."

"Um, well, I think you will, in fact, enjoy your stay with us. We have lots of amenities: indoor and outdoor pools, walking trails..."

"Good! A pool. You need our credit card?"

"Oh no, ma'am. It's all taken care of."

"Um...okay then. Where's our cabin?"

"It's just down the path on the right side of this building. Luckily, the rain has stopped just in time. Here are your key cards for the room. Yours is the last cabin at the end of the path, right beside the lake, and..."

"Great. Let's go, Adam."

"Give me a second. *Thank you*, Gabriel. Truly. Here's a little something for you."

"Thank you, sir! My pleasure."

"Lunch is at 1:00?"

"Yes, sir."

"Good. One it is then."

"Adam, why are you asking about lunch? I thought you were worried about getting to breakfast!"

"I am indeed. Looks like that's the dining room over there."

"Why did that man keep nodding at you? He kept looking at you the whole time I was the talking to him, like you were some sort of celebrity or something. How rude and sexist. I hate men like that. And, what the hell did you tip him for? That's his job!"

"It's customary to reward those in the service industry, dear. Here we are, finally. Looks like it's a buffet, and they haven't started the meeting yet. Let's put our jackets on the chairs at that table up front by the podium so we can hear and see everything. Then we can get in line and get something to eat. I'm starving!"

"Whatever."

"Eat a hearty breakfast, my dear. You never know when a meal might be your last."

The Keepers

It was the first day of spring when Dr. Celia Mayfield finally took a vacation to the destination she'd always dreamt of, literally. She hadn't known the actual location until just recently, not the state nor the city, but the place had called to her for years. Glimpses of events and people in her fragmented, recurring dream had changed from time to time, but not the landscape. She dreamt of a quaint cottage beside a white lighthouse overlooking a fishing village on the banks of a horseshoe-shaped bay.

The dream had spawned a fascination with lighthouses, and Celia began researching them while in high school. Over the years, she'd checked out hundreds of library books, visited several coastal areas, and searched the Internet hoping to stumble upon a posted photo of "the one." Finally, early one brisk March morning, she thought she had done just that. An hour later, her room was booked and she'd started making a to-do list of what she needed to get done before her trip, which included meeting with the Chair of the Psychology Department to finalize her teaching load for the following semester.

Celia had been a Psychology professor for nearly thirty years and had lived in Kentucky her whole life. She was the author of numerous textbooks and a frequent guest lecturer at institutions of higher learning across the country, which had aided in her lighthouse quest.

This particular spring semester, she had taken a sabbatical to finish another book, this one a work of fiction, but it wasn't going well. She'd stalled mid-chapter about twenty thousand words into the historical romance. After rereading what she'd written several times, she knew something was missing, something important, she just didn't know what.

Celia was tall with a curvy, buxom build that was fashionable in the '50s but now considered overweight. Her natural chestnut brown hair had begun to gray, so she'd opted to color it strawberry blonde, which suited her fair complexion.

Two lengthy marriages had produced two beautiful children, but little more. Her son, Stan, had married his high school sweetheart, found success as a graphic artist in Seattle, and was now the father of three rambunctious boys. His vivacious younger sister, Mandy, owned a thriving boutique in Texas and had become quite successful in marketing her handcrafted jewelry worldwide. Celia, meanwhile, was still landlocked in Kentucky. And at fifty-seven, retirement was quickly approaching. Relocation was foremost on her mind, which both excited and frustrated her. She had yet to find that quaint little cottage by the white lighthouse on the horseshoe bay.

She left on a Friday morning and drove straight through, arriving on a breezy early evening in Donner's Bay, North Carolina. When she exited the expressway, Celia became invigorated, despite her fatigue. Slowly winding her hybrid compact through the side streets and down the gentle slope of the hillside, she rounded a corner and came to the center of the picturesque village.

It was dinnertime and the sun was hanging low on the horizon. As she sat in the parking lot of the B&B where she had booked a room for the week, the panoramic view of the bay below took her breath away. The docks were still bustling with activity as fishermen hauled in their catches of the day, fishmongers made deals, and locals milled about. On the north side of the bay, setting on a high hill that gently sloped down to meet the Atlantic Ocean, was the cottage and lighthouse.

She sat for a moment staring up at it, and then excitedly grabbed her bags from the back seat and followed the brick pavers up to the front porch of the bed and breakfast. It was an inviting Colonial

Revival with white siding, black shutters, and a barn red double front door. A second floor balcony covered a lower front porch that spanned the width of the building. The black wooden rockers and small table and chair sets on the porch invited guests to gather and socialize. When Celia entered the inn, a petite young woman with unruly, bright red hair and purple horn-rimmed glasses greeted her.

"Welcome to Bayview Inn! How can I help you?"

"Hello. Celia Mayfield. I have a reservation."

"Oh yes, Ms. Mayfield. We have your room ready. Have a seat here and we'll get you checked in. I'm Junie." She motioned to a leather arm chair beside the burled walnut desk on the right of the foyer and Celia sat down. "Is this your first visit to Donner's Bay?"

"Yes. It looks like a lovely place."

"It is indeed," Junie said with another winning smile. "Our little town is filled with nice folks; plenty of activities; and awesome local shops and restaurants, including our own, of course," she added. "Plus, you can't beat the views!"

Celia laughed, captivated by the young woman's seemingly genuine enthusiasm. "Have you lived here long?" she asked as Junie recorded her credit card information and programmed her room key cards.

"Oh, about ten years now. I moved here from Colorado after I graduated to help my aunt and uncle when they opened the inn. I *love* it here!"

"Well that's great," Celia said. "Tell me, do you know much about the lighthouse and the little cottage beside it? I was hoping to get a closer look at it. Do they offer tours?"

"The lighthouse?" Junie asked, turning her head north, as though to look up at it, although no windows were within the sightline of her desk. "Um...Mr. and Mrs. Braden live in the cottage. They're the current keepers. Sweet older couple. We don't have any official tours I don't think, but I'm sure they would be happy to show it to you. Mrs. Braden loves to chat, at least that's my impression whenever I've seen her in town. Mr. Braden's quiet but nice enough. I figure he just gave up trying to get a word in," she added with a giggle.

Celia laughed. "Thanks for the info. I'll try to pay them a visit."

"Okay, you're all checked in. Let me show you to your room and tell you a little about Bayview," Junie said, standing and reaching for one of Celia's bags and then leading the way up the grand central staircase. "We serve breakfast in the back sunroom from 7:30 to 9:30 each morning, but there's coffee and pastries available in the front parlor by 6:30. They haven't opened the pool yet, but there's a hot tub on the south patio that you may enjoy, and it's available 24-7. Finally, our restaurant and bar, Smithy's, is in a wing off the back of the building. It's open to inn guests and the public from noon to 10:00 pm. They have excellent seafood dishes and the best steaks in town."

"Sounds promising. I'm starving."

Junie nodded. "Trust me, order the Surf & Turf. It's *awesome*," she said, and then continued her spiel. "We lock the main doors at 11:00 each night for your safety, but your key card will open them. If you would like us to clean your room, or if you need more towels or anything, just call or stop by the front desk here. We won't bother you otherwise."

"That sounds fine. Thank you."

"Okay then!" Junie beamed, "Here we are, lucky room number seven." She used one of the key cards, opened the door, and then handed the two cards to Celia. "Enjoy your stay, Ms. Mayfield, and let me know if there's anything at all I can do for you. I'll be here all week."

Celia thanked Junie again, closed the door, and then stood for a moment taking in the generously sized room filled with beautiful, upscale furnishings. A queen-size bed with a distressed white shutter headboard dominated the room. The spread had a muted coral background with subtle white and gray seahorses, starfish, and crab patterns. A low dresser with a TV on top was opposite the bed.

One side wall consisted entirely of a built-in unit: two small closets on either side of a cushioned bench beneath a small bay window. The bathroom entrance was on the opposite side wall.

Inside were a glass enclosed shower with a pebble floor and a vanity with a marble top.

Celia was amazed at how luxurious the room was for the price. It looked even better in person than in the photos on the B&B's website.

After unpacking, she made her way to Smithy's, where she ordered the Surf & Turf. It was delicious, just as Junie had promised. After dinner, she walked out to the large covered patio where a young man playing an acoustic guitar was performing soothing tunes.

Celia ordered a glass of merlot and took a seat at a small table near a patio heater. She chatted with a couple of friendly locals who sat at neighboring tables and enjoyed a relaxing, pleasurable evening. And that night, in the queen-size bed under the nautical comforter, Celia had the best night's sleep she'd had in what seemed like forever—a peaceful, dreamless sleep.

After breakfast the next morning, Celia layered a sweater over her T-shirt, grabbed her Nikon and shoulder bag, and left the inn. It was another breezy day, but the warm sun was shining brightly, and she spent hours roaming downtown streets.

The colorful awnings, hanging signs, and window decorations of the various shops provided wonderful backdrops for photos. She was amazed at how clean and well kempt the town was. Trimmed dwarf trees, lamp posts, benches, and flowerboxes adorned the wide sidewalks. Locals and visitors alike roamed the streets. And best of all, no one seemed stressed or in a hurry.

She enjoyed a bowl of delicious clam chowder for lunch at the Cozy Café down by the docks, and then stopped by the Donner's Bay Museum and Visitor's Center to inquire about the lighthouse. At both places, she saw an elderly man with thick, shoulder length, white hair. He was slightly heavy set and wore a red and black checked flannel shirt with jeans. She thought it just a coincidence seeing him at both places until he walked into an antique store while she was there later that afternoon.

The owner, Isabel, was telling Celia about the item she was interested in: a dainty silver chain with a lighthouse pendant. "You've chosen a lovely necklace. I acquired it from an estate sale last year. It supposedly belonged to the wife of the third lighthouse keeper, August Standish."

"Really?" Celia said, excited by her find. As soon as she spotted it in the glass display case, she was immediately drawn to it.

"Yes. Her name was Amanda. Local legend has it that she was the real keeper. It's said that August developed a fear of heights not long after he took up the post, perhaps after almost falling over the outer railing surrounding the lantern room.

"I'll bet she was a loyal and determined woman," Celia said absently as she traced her finger over the pendent.

Isabel looked at her for a moment. "Well, I suppose she probably was."

"Did they have children, do you know?"

"Two, I believe, a boy and a girl."

"Hmm," Celia said. After a moment, she took in a deep breath, and then looked up at Isabel and smiled. "Do you happen to know how old the lighthouse is?"

"You know, I'm not sure of the exact year it was built," Isabel admitted. "I need to find out. A few other customers have asked me that. I know it was sometime in the early 1800's."

"I stopped by the visitor's center to find out more about it, but it was busy so I didn't stay. Thought I'd go back later in the week. I'd love to learn about the history of the lighthouse and its former keepers. If I find out when it was first built, I'll let you know."

"Great! Thanks. I do know that the first keeper's house was made of stone. There are some ruins up there, a chimney and foundation that you can still see. His name was Jonathon something-or-other. The little keeper's cottage that's there now was built in the 1950's, I believe."

"Interesting. They need you over at the visitor's center," Celia said.

Isabel laughed. "Nah, I'm just a history buff. Sort of need to be if I'm going to run an antique store, right? I need to learn more about the lighthouse and its keepers myself, actually."

"Well, I absolutely love the necklace. I'll take it," she said, handing Isabel her credit card.

Celia instantly liked the shop owner. They were about the same age, and she felt comfortable talking to her. She wondered if they might become friends if she decided to retire in Donner's Bay. Celia realized that the older you got, the harder it was to make new friends. And she felt an immediate connection with Isabel, the way you sometimes do with new acquaintances, while others you immediately dislike for no apparent reason.

As Isabel was ringing up Celia's purchase, the white haired man Celia had seen earlier around town entered the shop.

"Now here's the fella you need to talk to," Isabel said to Celia. "Hello, Buck!"

"Afternoon, Ms. Isabel."

"Celia, this is Buck Braden, our current lighthouse keeper. Buck, this is Celia Mayfield. It's her first visit to our little town, and she's interested in the history of the lighthouse."

"I 'spect she is." He smiled at Celia and nodded.

Celia smiled back but found his comment a little odd. She realized that lighthouses intrigued many people, though, and imagined he'd been bothered quite a lot by vacationers.

"I've seen you around town today," she said. "Seems we've been visiting many of the same places."

"So it seems, ma'am," he said.

"Well, I don't want to bother you. I was just curious about the lighthouse and cottage, just as many visitors are, I expect."

"No bother. Mayor's been talking about giving tours during the peak tourist season."

"That would be a great idea, I think. It would probably bring in quite a bit of revenue for the town," Celia said and looked down for a moment, a little embarrassed, and then back at Mr. Braden. "I would love to get a closer look at it myself. I've...I've been searching for a particular lighthouse, you see, one I've had a recurring dream about for many years. I know that sounds strange," she quickly added, "but I swear it's true."

"I 'spect so," was all Mr. Braden said again with a wry smile.

"I wouldn't want to impose," she hurried on, "but I'd be willing to pay for a brief tour. I...I just need to know if it's the one in my dreams. The whole area—the town, the bay, the lighthouse—it all looks just like what I've been dreaming of. It's been haunting me!" Celia laughed nervously. "That sounds crazy when I say it out loud."

"No it doesn't." Isabel reached across the counter and gave Celia's hand a little pat to reassure her. "I had a recurring dream once, back in my younger days, about Elvis. And that's all I'm willing to tell about that," she added.

All three laughed. Celia appreciated Isabel trying to put her at ease.

"Me and the Mrs. will be home tomorrow," Buck said. "Say about noon? Will that do?"

"Oh, yes! That would be great. Thank you!" Celia said.

"Isabel, you get Harry to come watch the shop for you and come on up with Ms. Celia. Show her the way. Tandy baked a chocolate cake this morning, and she's making shepherd's pies for dinner tonight. I'm sure there will be plenty of both left over for lunch tomorrow."

"Sounds yummy! We'll be there. Okay with you, Celia? I haven't seen Tandy in a few weeks. We need to catch up."

"That would be nice," Celia said, relieved that Isabel was going with her.

The following day, Celia went into town early and stopped by the florist for a bouquet of spring flowers, and then headed to Isabel's antique shop. She met Isabel's husband, Harry, who was a tall, wiry fellow with a perpetual smile and youthful, bright blue eyes. He told her that he had just opened a new micro-brewery with his brother and invited her to visit while she was in town. Celia liked him instantly, just as she had Isabel. She wished him well with his new business venture and promised to stop by.

Leaving the shop in her husband's capable hands, Isabel drove them up to the lighthouse in her Suburban. Celia enjoyed the ride and learned more about the area from Isabel as she drove. As they approached the lighthouse, the area became more remote, with fewer and fewer houses along the road. When the cottage came into view, Celia gasped.

"I can't believe it! This is it! It's the exact cottage in my dreams!"

"Really? Are you sure?"

"Positive! There's the picket fence, blue shutters, split Dutch front door, and even the bright red porch swing...everything! It's just like in my dreams. Sorry, Isabel, but I'm just so excited to finally find it. And there are the brightly painted little sheds! See?" She pointed to the corner of a shed peeking out behind the cottage. "They are almost always in my dreams, and there are five of them in a row with a little garden patch in front of each one! I can't see that from here, of course, but I'll bet you they're there."

"How weird," Isabel whispered reverently, just a little spooked. "But cool!" she added quickly, not wanting Celia to think that she meant that *she* was weird, just the situation. "I think there *are* five, if I remember correctly. How could you possibly know that? How could you be dreaming of a place you've never seen before?"

"I have absolutely no idea. This is my first visit to North Carolina. My parents didn't bring me here when I was little or anything like that. No movies were ever filmed here that I could find; I just recently checked the Internet for that. I'm just...just stumped. But I'm relieved too, you know? I think it would be creepier if I kept dreaming about a place that *didn't* exist."

"Maybe you lived here in a former life," Isabel said with a little laugh, "if you believe in that sort of thing."

Celia nodded and then shrugged. "Actually, it's as good a theory as any."

When Isabel pulled up to the front of the cottage and parked, Buck and Tandy stepped out of the front door and waved to them. Neither Celia nor Isabel noticed when Tandy excitedly grabbed her husband's hand and gave it a squeeze.

As they walked onto the front porch, Isabel introduced the women and Celia handed Tandy the bouquet of flowers she'd bought in town. Tandy's eyes lit up. She thanked Celia and turned back into the house to hunt for a vase while Buck ushered the ladies into their home.

Celia was surprised by the modern, updated layout and décor. The living, dining and kitchen areas were open concept with a vaulted ceiling. The walls were a crisp white shiplap, decorated with architectural finds and artwork in shades of sandy browns and ocean blues, with splashes of yellow and navy here and there. To the left, there was an opening that led to a short hallway with a full bath between two bedrooms.

Buck showed them to the kitchen where Tandy was fussing with the flowers at the sink. "Come sit at the table, ladies."

"We're so glad you two came for lunch," Tandy said, bringing the low, round vase of flowers to the table and sitting it in the center. "We'll tell you what we can about the lighthouse, Celia. Buck says you're very interested in the place, that you've even had dreams about it. Is that right?"

"Yes, I have. I know it sounds odd. And I want to thank you so much for your hospitality."

"Oh, it's no bother at all. How about some iced tea? Isabel, tea for you?"

Both Celia and Isabel said yes to the tea and Tandy brought glasses for everyone to the table. While they chatted about how lovely the cottage was, Tandy took individual servings of shepherd's pie out of the oven. As they ate, Buck gave a cursory overview of the history of the Donner's Bay lighthouse.

"It was built in 1837, the last year our seventh president, Andrew Jackson, was in office," he began. "It was one of the first modern lighthouses in this area and is still considered state-of-the-art. It had a first order Fresnel lens in the lantern room, which has been updated over the years. The sturdy conical shape, with a fifty-seven foot deep foundation that sits on bedrock, has kept her standing strong all these years. The steel reinforced brick and stone base is seventy-seven feet high from the ground to the lantern room, and its light is visible for over seventeen nautical miles. There have been only six official keepers. I'm the sixth, although Tandy tends to her as much as I do. The next keeper will be lucky number seven."

"Lucky number seven," Celia said slowly, trying to remember who had recently said that same phrase to her.

"All lived long, happy lives, and are peaceful and content here," Tandy added.

"They *are* or *were*?" Celia chuckled.

"Oh lighthouse keepers never leave their posts, dear."

Buck nodded in agreement. "It's the town. Always been prosperous. Always good keepers," he said between the last bites of his shepherd's pie, ignoring Celia's look of astonishment. "Good pie too, my dear, as always."

"Tandy's one of the best cooks in the bay," Isabel said. "You should see what she can do with seafood. Her low country boil is the best I've ever had."

"I have no doubt about that. This is absolutely delicious," Celia said. "Really good seasoning, and the beef is so tender." She then tried to shift the conversation back to the comment Tandy had made. "So, do you..."

"Oh, Isabel's just trying to butter me up in hopes of an invite to dinner," Tandy said with a laugh, interrupting Celia.

"Wouldn't say no," Isabel admitted. "Harry says I'm an awful cook, so I'm sure he'd appreciate a reprieve."

"I'm sure your Harry's been getting plenty of nutrients from all of that micro-brew he's been testing," Tandy joked, which got a laugh from all. Tandy then gave her husband a quick look and added, "Tell you what, I'm going over to Jon's in the morning." To Celia she said, "That's our son. He's the best lawyer in Donner's Bay," she added with a wink. "I'll do a bit of shopping while I'm in town and then make that low country boil for you all tomorrow night if Celia will come a little early and help me. Isabel, you bring dessert, and get Harry to bring us some of that new wheat brew he's been talking about. How does that sound?"

"Sounds great!" Isabel and Celia said in unison, causing another round of laughter.

"It's settled then," Tandy said as she got up and gathered their bowls. Now, who's ready for some chocolate cake?"

At Celia's request, Buck revealed more about the former keepers as they all enjoyed generous slices of Tandy's delicious dessert. As Buck talked, the different timelines and keepers came to life. She thought Junie was right, Buck didn't talk much, but when he did, it was clear that he was a gifted storyteller.

His words weaved together people and events with fragments of her dreams, bringing them alive. She could almost see the Civil War skirmish that destroyed the first keeper's house, smell the fire that destroyed the second one, and hear the raging waves that damaged the lighthouse during hurricane Hugo in 1989.

Through it all, the keepers survived, rebuilt, repaired, and carried on. Buck told them that in the 90's, there was talk, and quite a bit of pressure, to turn the lighthouse over to the Coast Guard to operate, but the locals and state politicians won the debate and the lighthouse operation remained in the hands of private keepers.

When they had finished their dessert, Isabel said she should be getting back to help Harry close up the shop. As they walked to the door, Celia told them that she had already fallen in love with Donner's Bay and might one day move there when she retired.

"Why, you're too young yet to consider retiring!" Tandy insisted. "Maybe you just need a change of occupations. Is there a Mr. Mayfield, dear, if you don't mind my asking?"

Celia laughed. "No, it's just me. Married and divorced twice. Guess I'm not cut out for it."

"Pshaw, maybe you just haven't met your match," Tandy whispered conspiratorially with a wink.

"Uh oh, now you've done it," Isabel said chuckling as she pulled on Celia's arm, steering her out of the cottage's front door and onto the porch. "Tandy is the town matchmaker!"

"Oh dear!" Celia laughed and waved goodbye to the couple. "Thank you again for lunch and we'll see you tomorrow!"

The Bradens waved back. "I 'spect so," Buck said after the ladies got back into the Suburban and started down the drive.

"Um...I 'spect," Tandy agreed.

The following evening, Celia enjoyed her second visit to the cottage and another meal with her new friends. She arrived early to help Tandy fix dinner and learned her secret recipe for low country boil with sausage, shrimp, crab, potatoes and corn.

She got acquainted with Harry a bit more and liked his quick wit and infectious laugh, as well as his wheat beer. Celia didn't know much about micro-breweries or starting a small business, but she learned quite a bit about both from Harry that night.

She also met the Braden's son, Jon, who joined them for dinner and gave them a quick tour of the lighthouse. He was tall with a stocky build like his father, but had a mischievous grin and outgoing personality like his mother. He was an instantly likeable fellow, and as it was with Isabel, Celia felt she'd known him for years after only a few hours.

After dinner, the three couples leisurely roamed the grounds. They started with the keeper's sheds directly behind the cottage. Each seven-by-seven foot shed was brightly painted a different color, and each had a wooden plaque on the door with the name of a former keeper on it. They were lined up in a row with about three feet between them.

The little garden plots in front of each shed were raised beds, seven-by-seven also, with gravel paths between them that led to the shed doors. Celia noted how neat and tidy the little gardens were, freshly tilled and planted with new annuals. Daffodils and various perennial bulbs were already sprouting in some of the beds, eagerly welcoming spring. Jon smiled and told her that the keepers wouldn't have it any other way.

As they walked to each shed, Buck and Tandy told them a little about each keeper and his family, some of which even Jon had not heard before. It was the first time Isabel and Harry had seen the sheds up close, and they also enjoyed hearing the history of the former residents. Celia thought of Isabel's theory when Tandy mentioned that Amanda Standish's maiden name was the same as her own: Mayfield.

The rest of the week passed quickly for Celia. She bought souvenirs for her kids and grandkids, took many more photos, visited Harry's micro-brewery, and spent a couple of hours watching the fishermen at the dock. She enjoyed watching them work, and the bobbing of the boats on the water was mesmerizing and calming.

One rainy afternoon, she helped Isabel package up three large pieces that she'd sold online. And one morning, she even contacted a real estate agent and toured two homes on the market later that afternoon, but neither quite suited her. Still, she felt more and more at home in the little coastal village with each passing day. She was sure her retirement home was somewhere close by.

On her last day in Donner's Bay, Jon left a note for her at the B&B, inviting her to dinner. He picked her up at six and they drove about thirty minutes up the coast, and then crossed on a ferry to Mayson Island, home to a resort with an award-winning, upscale restaurant.

After dinner, Jon retrieved a blanket from his SUV and they sat on the beach below the restaurant. Celia thought life couldn't get much better: wine, a good meal, and an evening filled with comfortable conversation with an interesting man in the place of her dreams.

When they arrived back at the inn, Jon asked Celia to sit tight for a minute, and then he retrieved a plant in a bright yellow pot from the back seat floorboard. He got back into the driver's seat and handed the plant to Celia.

"It's from my parents."

"Periwinkles! How sweet of them," she said, and then noticed the note card stuck into the side of the pot. She read it aloud. "'Dear Celia, Periwinkles are our favorites, and yellow is our favorite color.'" She looked up at Jon, who was smiling at her ruefully. "Well, they're lovely.

Periwinkles are one of my favorite flowers too. Please thank them for me."

"When you return, you can thank them yourself. How soon will that be, do you suppose? Soon, I hope. We've all grown quite fond of you over this past week, Ms. Celia."

"What a sweet thing to say, Jon," she said and patted his arm. "I've enjoyed every minute of my vacation here at Donner's Bay. It...it feels like home, like it would be a wonderful place to retire. I've even talked with a real estate agent already," she added with a laugh.

"Oh, you won't need one. I know just the property for you."

"Really?" she asked excitedly. "Where?"

"It's not on the market yet." He paused, stared out of the windshield for a moment, and then added solemnly, "It should be soon though." He then quickly looked back at Celia. "Give me your contact information and I'll get in touch as soon as it's available if you're really interested."

"I am!" She wrote her number and address on the back of a receipt and gave it to him, and then asked him to share it with Isabel as well. "She's been so kind and helpful to me," she said. "I'd like to keep in touch."

"Come back to us soon, Celia," Jon said, and then reached over to give her a kiss on the cheek and a hug.

She smiled at him, got out with her pot of periwinkles, and headed toward the front door of the B&B. She heard Jon back up and pull away as she walked along the brick pavers. When she reached the porch, she turned and looked up at the beacon of light sweeping over the Atlantic Ocean from the lighthouse on the cliff and felt its pull, as though it was searching for her.

Two years later:

Celia was watering the flowers in front of the new, bright yellow shed one sunny Saturday when she heard Isabel and Harry coming up the long drive. She walked to the corner of the cottage and waved to them, letting them know she was out back. They parked and then walked around back to join her.

"Need a hand?" Isabel called.

"Sure! My kinfolk's plot still needs to be watered. I've finished all the rest," Celia said.

Isabel fetched a watering can from the back porch and filled it with the hose at the corner of the cottage. Harry then took it to the garden plot in front of the lime green Standish shed and began watering the day lilies and variegated hostas.

As they finished the watering chore out back, Junie and her fiancé, Alex, pulled up in his Land Rover. Jon came out the front door of the cottage to greet them. Everyone has come for dinner. Celia has made Tandy's famous low country boil and cherry pie for dessert.

The little keeper's cottage was filled with lively discussion and laughter that evening. Much of the conversation centered around the success of Celia's historical romance novel and the addition she and Jon were building on the side of the cottage.

The novel was selling really well, and she had started on a second book, one based more on historical fact than fiction, perhaps. The construction crew had just finished the drywall on the addition, so everyone took a tour of the new space: two generously sized bedrooms and a second full bath.

"They're coming to paint on Monday," Celia said excitedly.

"I love the bunk room!" Junie said, commenting on the back bedroom with its four built-in bunks, two on either side of a tall window that overlooked the brightly colored sheds. "Those grandkids of yours will love it!"

"Hope so," Celia said. "Stan and Jill are bringing them in a couple of weeks for an end-of-summer vacation before school starts back. I think Mandy will be able to come too, and there will be plenty of room now that we have four bedrooms. I'm anxious for all of them to visit," she added with a smile.

After their guests had left that evening, Jon helped Celia check the lighthouse, and then retired to his recliner in front of the TV. Celia was tired and went straight to bed. Before lying down, she sat on the side of the bed and removed the necklace she'd bought at Isabell's shop. She studied it, thinking of all that had happened since that day. She laid the necklace on the nightstand and then opened the drawer below and pulled out the letter she'd received six months after her first visit to Donner's Bay. It was from Jon's law firm, informing her that both of the Braden's had passed away and left cottage to her in their wills. She then opened the handwritten note that Jon had slipped into the envelope before mailing the legal document.

Dear Celia,

Mom and Dad passed peacefully in their sleep on the same night. I found them the next morning. They were lying in bed on their backs, holding hands. And I swear they had smiles on their faces. I'm feeling a little lost without them, but it's a comfort to know they are still close by, watching over the lighthouse until you arrive.

I would have called, but in accordance with their wishes, there was no formal visitation or funeral service. They were cremated and I have their ashes in urns, for now. They were lucky to have lived happy, healthy, active lives into their early nineties. But they had grown tired, Celia, and were just waiting patiently for you.

Please come as soon as you can to tend to the paperwork. You and I are the only heirs. And in case you're concerned, I helped Mom and Dad write their wills and knew of their intentions.

They left their belongings and a little cash to me, but it is not for me to tend to the lighthouse and sheds. These are yours, as they should be, although I'd be happy to help.

Please say you'll come back to Donner's Bay, and that you'll stay and take up the post as the 7th keeper. We've all missed you. I've missed you, Celia.

We'll start construction on their shed and garden plot once you arrive and settle in. Then we'll have a little ceremony and lay Mom and Dad to rest among the periwinkles.

Sincerely yours,
Jon

Celia folded the letter, put it back into her nightstand, and walked to the window. She looked out at the cottages in the back yard and could see, under the moonlight, all of the former keepers milling around their gardens, chatting with each other. Buck and Tandy looked up at her window and waved. Celia waved back and smiled, knowing that she and Jon would join them one day. Lighthouse keepers never leave their posts.

Twenty-two years later:

A young man came calling at Jon & Celia's door one day. He was new to the area and a handyman. He said he was told that they might need some help around the place.

Jon smiled and told the young man that they could, in fact, use his help. He grabbed the cane he kept perched by the front door and showed the young man around the property, pointing out a few odd jobs that needed to be done.

The young man was eager to help and got started on one simple job right then. When he finished, he came back to the cottage to have Jon check the work he had done. It exceeded Jon's expectations, so he lined up a few more jobs with the young man, and then invited him to stay for dinner. Celia had made baked spaghetti and German chocolate cake.

The handyman eagerly accepted the invitation, longing for a home cooked meal. After he left that evening, Celia told Jon that this man was the one.

Jon smiled, nodded, and said, "I 'spect so."

He went to the bookshelf beside the fireplace and removed a stack of books. Behind it was a small safe built into the wall that they never kept locked. He opened the safe and retrieved an old, leather-bound journal, and then sat in his worn recliner in front of the fireplace.

He put on his reading glasses and picked up the pencil lying on top of the newspaper's daily crossword puzzle. Gently, he opened the journal and turned to the last entry. He reread the biography of the seventh lighthouse keeper and smiled, satisfied with what he and Celia had written about themselves. He then wrote the handyman's name a few lines below their own entry: Nathaniel ("Nathan") Humpfrey.

"Did you put his name in the book?" Celia called from the kitchen.

"I've penciled it in," he called back. "We'll put it in ink once we're sure."

"Okay, but I'm sure." She brought his cup of tea and sat it on the side table.

Jon smiled. "I love you, Celia Braden."

"Love you back, old man," she replied as she returned to the kitchen.

He chuckled, closed the journal, and gently ran his fingers over the embossed title on the cover:

The Rightful and True Descendants
of the English Colony of Roanoke Island, Faithful
Keepers of the Donner Light, In God's Trust.

Mr. Hoppy and the Pliers

He handed Amy an ice scraper, a box of Kleenex, and a pair of pliers. She looked at the items a moment, shook her head in exasperation, and then tossed all three through the open window of the driver's side door. The box of Kleenex landed on the console. The other two items landed in the passenger side floorboard.

"Did you put the jumper cables in the trunk?" he asked.

"Yep, along with the de-icer, Fix-a-Flat thingy, and Bungee cord."

Amy perched on the metal work bench stool in the garage and swiveled from side to side while she waited for her father to finish his inspection. He continued to fuss with the slightly used, fire engine red Nissan for another fifteen minutes, and then finally handed her the car keys.

She had traded in her first car, an old Chevy Malibu, for the shiny import because her parents had insisted that she get something more reliable before driving over a thousand miles from their home in Louisville to her friend's house in Denver. Amy was a strong supporter of buying American made products, but her parents thought foreign made cars lasted longer. And since they offered to pay half of the price of the Nissan, she didn't argue.

Janice, who had been Amy's best friend since grade school, had moved to Denver the year before, right after graduating from U of L with a business degree. She landed a plum entry-level position with a marketing firm right away and had already received a promotion. When Amy graduated with a degree in accounting the next semester, she applied for a few positions around Louisville, but no luck.

That's when Janice began urging her to come for a visit and to apply for some jobs in the Denver area. With this goal in mind, Amy stayed with her folks and took a full-time job as a server at a local upscale bar and grill. On one of her days off, she helped her uncle with the bookkeeping for his ranch. After only six months, she'd saved up enough for her half of the new car plus the trip out west. She was anxious to see her friend, and to see what Denver had to offer.

As Amy watched and swiveled, her father performed the final tasks on his automotive checklist: headlights, seat belts, and windshield wipers. All were in perfect working order. He smiled and nodded to her, signaling that he was pleased with the inspection, and then went to the workbench and pulled a brown paper sack from a shelf above the Dewalt chop saw.

"Okay. I think you're all set," he declared.

"Fantastic!" she said with a sigh of relief, hopping off of the stool. "I need to go over to Judy's and get my sweater back that she borrowed last week. I won't have time in the morning before I leave. Oh, and I need to fill up with gas, too."

"Okay then, you're all set," he repeated. "There's just one more thing." He opened the bag and pulled out the small, pink and white, stuffed bunny rabbit he had given his only child for her third birthday. "This is your mascot. Keep him on the dashboard. He'll keep you safe."

She took the rabbit and hugged him tightly to her chest. "Mr. Hoppy! Ah Dad, how sweet! I haven't seen this old rabbit in years." She gave her father a big hug, thanked him, and told him she loved him. "I'll be back soon. Promise."

He nodded and smiled, but couldn't speak. His little girl wasn't three anymore, but she was still just as fragile and innocent in his mind.

Twenty-four hours later, Amy was just west of Kansas City on I-70. It was late and traffic had thinned considerably. Her back was stiff and she was getting sleepy, so she decided to stop for the night when she saw a sign for a Holiday Inn Express at the next exit.

She tapped the brake to release the cruise control, but maintained her speed, which was just slightly over the limit. She looked up into the rearview mirror at the lights of a semi that seemed to be approaching fast. *He must be flying*, she thought as her eyes kept darting from the road to the mirror. Amy sped up a little, willing her exit to appear, but it was still several miles down the highway.

The semi's headlights got brighter and brighter in the rearview mirror, and when she looked into the mirror again, she saw that it was right behind her, almost on her bumper.

She maintained her speed and became angry when the driver wouldn't go around her. She waited, planning to try to memorize his plate number when he did finally decide to pass her. When he didn't pass, she decided to move over into the left lane herself and just let him get ahead of her. She put on her blinker, changed lanes, and slowed down. But the semi stayed in the right lane and slowed to match her speed. Then, without warning, it swerved toward her.

Amy panicked. She braked hard and moved off onto the shoulder of the road, somehow managing to keep the Nissan under control. The semi was in front of her now, so she swerved hard to the right, getting off of the shoulder and back into the left lane of the highway. When she did, Mr. Hoppy flew off of the dashboard and landed in the passenger seat with his back up against the door. His unblinking, plastic eyes were fixed on her. But she didn't notice. She couldn't take her eyes from the road and the semi in front of her. She wouldn't have been able to see his penetrating stare in the darkness of the car's interior anyway.

She drove slowly, well under the speed limit, keeping the semi in front of her. *The exit has to be just up ahead*, she though. And just then, the semi braked in front of her. Its crimson taillights glowed like faceless demon eyes in the night.

Amy slowed to nearly a stop, not wanting to try and pass the semi, knowing that the driver would try to force her off the road again. She looked in the rearview mirror, hoping to see the headlights of another car approaching, but the road was black behind her. When she looked back out of the windshield, she saw that the semi had stopped, and she slammed on her brakes, coming to a stop just a few feet from the rig.

Her heart pounded and she gripped the steering wheel tightly, trying to decide what to do. Suddenly, it came to her. She looked down to the gearshift in the console and was about to put the car in reverse, and then go forward again as fast as she could to get around the stopped semi, when the window of her driver's side door shattered.

Safety glass rained down on her. She lunged sideways, the gearshift gouging into her ribs, and her foot came off of the brake pedal. She screamed when the driver's side door flew open and the semi driver jumped in, but not before the Nissan bumped into the back of the semi. He backed the car up and pulled it off onto the left shoulder as she scrambled to sit up.

Amy turned her back to the man behind the wheel of her car and fumbled for the passenger door handle. She got it open and swung her feet out, but was not quite quick enough. He grabbed her long blonde braid with one hand and the back of her white tank top with the other, hauling her back inside the car. Her head hit the top of the door opening hard and she almost passed out. And then she felt the semi driver trying to pull her out of the driver's side door.

Energized by a fresh wave of panic, she flipped onto her stomach and began kicking at the man, whose hands still gripped her ankles tightly. She stretched out on the front seats, clawing frantically, trying to find something to hold onto. Then she spotted the pair of pliers lying in the floorboard.

She grabbed them and quickly flipped onto her back again. The unexpected movement loosened her assailant's grip a little, and Amy sat up quickly, bringing the weapon in her right hand down hard on the bridge of his nose. The pliers connected squarely with their intended target and the man grunted. He released his grip on her legs and stumbled backward.

Amy watched the scene before her play out as though in slow motion under the illumination of the Nissan's dome light. The semi driver's arms began to cartwheel as the heel of his right boot sunk into the gravel and vegetation on the side of the road and he tumbled backward, down the slope and into the median.

Amy blinked, dropped the pliers, slammed her door shut, and put the car in reverse. Without even looking to see if any other cars were around, she swerved into the right lane and floored it, leaving the semi behind at the top of a hill. Less than two miles ahead, she saw the lights of the exit and put on her blinker.

She didn't rise until after noon the next day. It had been a long night, and what little sleep she got was restless and filled with frightening dreams of being chased in the darkness.

As she gathered the few items she'd brought into the motel, she reviewed what she'd told the police the night before, wondering if she'd left anything out. She could only remember two numbers of the semi's license plate number, and could only vaguely remember what she saw of the driver's face in the shadows. But she did remember a portion of the logo on the side of the truck that filled her passenger side window when the driver had tried to run her off the road. It was a snow-capped mountain peak.

Amy checked out of the Holiday Inn, threw her purse into the front seat, and then tossed her overnight bag in the trunk with her suitcase. She got in and checked the fuel gauge, which showed only a quarter of a tank remaining, so she planned to fill up and grab a bite to eat before getting back on the road again.

As she reached for the seatbelt, her cell phone rang. It was one of the police officers she'd spoken to the night before. He informed her that they had caught the semi driver in Junction City.

When she asked if he was sure, the officer told her that they were positive. The man had scratches on his hands and face from the tumble he took into the median, and a nice purple bruise was starting to form on his abdomen from where she'd kicked him, the officer said. On top of that, there were fire engine red paint marks on the back of his rig. Best of all, the young officer proudly announced, it only took fifteen minutes of questioning before the semi driver actually confessed.

Amy was so relieved. She thanked him for the call, and then thanked him again when he told her she wouldn't have to go to the police station to identify the semi driver. He said her statement from the night before would be sufficient, and that if they needed anything else, they would contact her.

She ended the call, put her head back on the headrest, closed her eyes, and exhaled deeply. She was relieved that the driver had been arrested, knowing that his next attempted attack might have been successful.

She had started the car and put it in reverse when her cell phone rang again, so she put it back into park and answered the call. This time, it was the HR department of a large company in Louisville. She had applied for a position in their Accounts Payable Department, and they were calling to schedule an interview.

After she hung up this time, Amy sat for a moment, and then smiled, backed out of the parking spot, and drove to the car dealership across the street. It took just over an hour for her to trade the red Nissan sedan in for a royal blue Buick Enclave.

By 3:00 that afternoon, she was on her way back to Louisville. Mr. Hoppy sat in the center of the new dashboard, with a pair of silver pliers in his lap.

A New Estate

The driveway seemed much shorter, the house much smaller, but many things were just as I remembered them. It was a square, single story dwelling built on a gently sloping hill with a walk-out basement in back. Large double doors graced the center of the home in front, and giant poplar trees anchored each corner. Floor to ceiling glass spanned across the front and back, capped with a hipped roof where Dad put the glowing Santa and reindeer each Christmas.

It was a beautiful home of mid-century architecture that sat in the center of ten acres of land just outside Atlanta. One of a kind, it was conceived from my parents' imagination, and then grew from their toil and sweat nearly fifty years ago.

I continued down the straight gravel driveway, parked in the double carport in back, and then climbed the few steps to the wide catwalk that extended up over the sunken patio and led to the back door. I stopped midway and looked out over the land. Memories came flooding back, bright and vivid, of days spent laughing and playing in the yard, singing and dancing on the catwalk, helping Dad with chores, and Mom teaching me to bake cookies.

Not long ago, on a brisk day in January, I had told Dad how much I loved and missed the old house. It was just idle chat, an attempt to take his mind off the pain and fatigue he had endured for so long during his battle with a host of health problems. But he knew I was sincere. I told him I wanted to build another one just like it someday and asked if he still had the blueprints. He just laughed at that.

"Blueprints? Not for that house, Melanie," he said. "We just built it a little at a time. Bought the land with every penny of our savings. Bought the cement block for the basement walls with my Christmas bonus that year. We'd save up, and when we had enough, we'd buy something else, whatever was needed next. Took us two years piecing it together like that, but we made it. Moved in just twelve days before you were born," he added with obvious pride.

"I heard you and Uncle Charlie talking about the exterior walls one time," I said, glad to see him smile. "There isn't any wood in them, right?"

"Nope, not a splinter! They're what they call cavity walls. The two side walls are eight inch masonry block with red brick veneer on the outside and fancy white brick that Wanda Jean picked out on the inside. Your momma loved that brick," he remembered and chuckled. "There's a three inch air space, or cavity, between the block and the interior brick. All told, they're about eighteen inches thick. The front and back walls of the house are made of four-by-eight insulated glass panels in wood frames. We made the frames ourselves and had a glass man come out to custom make the panels. The top ones were cut to fit the slope of the roof, and it gave him fits trying to get them just right, I'll tell ya."

Dad turned to stare out of the hospital window, still smiling. No doubt he was envisioning the old home place, seeing it when it was under construction, seeing himself as a strong, young man building it.

"Do you remember how high the roof was, Dad?" I asked gently, trying to hold back the tears. I hated seeing him lying in that hospital bed, daydreaming of days gone by. But he seemed to enjoy talking about the old days, so I encouraged him to tell me more.

"Oh sure," he said quickly, turning back toward me and readjusting himself in the bed a little. "The roof was a low pitch design, if you recall. It was made of heavy tongue and groove pine laid over massive solid beams and rafters. The ceiling timbers were varnished to a high shine. The peak rose to a height of 20 feet, sloping to 10 feet at the walls. There were oversized double front doors and a heated slate foyer, too. Do you remember that, Mel?"

I nodded and smiled.

"He turned his head to look out of the hospital window again and added slowly, "We wanted something solid, you see, something that would last forever." Then he turned back to me and added brightly, "I can't believe I've made it long enough to see a new millennium."

"I know! It's fascinating how much has changed since you were born, isn't it? Think of how many new inventions you've seen, how the world has changed."

"It has changed so much," he said slowly and closed his eyes. The morphine drip had dispensed another dose, making him drowsy. "You'll have to tell me what the 21st century was like when you get to Heaven, Mel."

I promised I would, told him I loved him, and hugged him for the last time.

I'm sure the conversation we had that day is the reason why Dad left his life savings to my brother and the house and personal property to me. He had no way of knowing that I needed the money much more than my little brother, who had become quite a successful businessman.

Although I'd built up a fairly good career myself as a real estate agent in Florida, the economy had taken a nose dive, so sales had slowed way down the past couple of years. And my recent divorce had not left me as well off as Dad may have assumed. Instead, it left me broke and broken hearted. But I never told him any of this. Now, I had come home to heal, and to attempt to start over.

As I turned to walk the rest of the way over the catwalk to the back door, the scent of lilacs engulfed me. Apparently, the lilac bushes were still on the side of the house where Mom and I had planted them the year before she died in a car accident when I was eighteen.

I stopped once more, leaned against the railing and lifted my face to the sun, trying to erase the sad memory from my mind. With my eyes still closed, I let the warm spring breeze wash over me, cleansing my mind, settling my emotions.

I focused my senses to take in all of the things I loved about the place but had almost forgotten. I heard the ducks on the lake behind the old school across the road, the whinny of the neighbor's horses in their stable, and the wind chimes above the back door. Memories of the happy childhood days I had spent there came flooding back to me.

When I opened my eyes once more, I could see the schoolhouse just down the road. There was a bright red sports car parked in front of it and I wondered who could be visiting the old school.

It had been built in the 1800's by a man whose wife's name was Mary. They lived next door in a stone cottage and she taught at the schoolhouse for many years. The place became known as Mary's Elementary.

It was supposedly the last one room schoolhouse still in use in Georgia back when I attended first through fifth grade there. They closed it the following year, so I was among the last of its students.

Dad bought the property several years ago when there was talk of tearing the school down. He had planned to restore the buildings and open an antique and gift shop. Tourism had increased in the area in recent years, and it was on a main road between two cities, so it was a good idea, but he never got around to it before he got sick.

I turned to walk on toward the back door, trying not to notice how badly the catwalk needed painting, or how many paver stones were missing from the patio below. "Well, the key works, and there's no horrible smell so far. That's a plus," I said aloud as I opened the weathered door and stepped into the home where I grew up. It was like stepping back in time.

The main floor actually didn't look so bad. The carpet was a mess, the kitchen cabinets needed refinishing, and the paper on the tall semicircle wall behind the top of the spiral staircase that led to the basement had peeled part way down from the top. I knew that just these minor repairs would cost a fortune, and I hadn't even checked the condition of the furnace, plumbing, or roof yet. But I was in love with the house all over again.

As I walked on toward the massive stone fireplace that separated the kitchen and dining areas from the large living room, someone came in behind me so quietly that I was unaware of their presence.

"Hello there."

I gasped and turned to face the intruder. "Oh my goodness, you scared me to death!"

"Sorry, I didn't mean to startle you," he said with a concerned look on his face. "The back door was standing open, and...I saw your car pull in the drive when I was over at Mary's Elementary, and...I'm really sorry."

I regained my composure, but my heart was still beating fast. "Oh, I'm fine. I was just off in another world and didn't hear you come in. You were over at the old school?"

"Yes, I was told that Mr. James owns the property now, and I came over to speak to him about it. You...you wouldn't happen to be his daughter by any chance, would you?" he asked hesitantly.

"Yes, I am. Sorry, I'm not being very hospitable today, am I? I'm Melanie James, and you're?"

"Roger," he said slowly, smiling. "Roger Jennings. Ring any bells? It was a long time ago, but..."

"You're kidding! Roger Jennings?"

"Yep, older, heavier, and balder, but it's me. The years have been good to you, though."

"Thanks for the compliment, but I've changed plenty, too. And you're not bald, you know. Your hair's still that gorgeous shade of blonde that drove all the little girls wild!"

"Even you?" he asked teasingly.

"Oh definitely. I had a major crush on you in fifth grade, you know."

"Well, I do remember us sort of...discovering each other one day when we were out by the old tree fort during recess," he said, looking down at the awful carpet with a grin on his face.

"Oh, the tree fort! I remember that." The big trunk of the tree had split at the bottom and the lower branches bowed out, and then bent back toward the center. It resembled the palm and fingers of a cupped hand. "Was that your first kiss too?" I asked, amused by his embarrassment.

"Yes, it was. Funny how you always remember your first kiss." He smiled again and looked at me with gorgeous blue eyes that still seemed bright and playful.

"Yeah, and probably your last one too!"

We both laughed, but the laughter died down strangely, like the wisecrack had hit too close to home for both of us.

"I hope your dad doesn't mind that I was poking around the old school. I came out to visit my mom today and thought I'd dig up some old memories while I was here, you know?

"Oh, no problem. Do your parents still live just up the road?" I asked.

"Mom does. Dad passed away last year, so my sisters and I try to visit as often as we can."

"I'm so sorry to hear about your dad. Actually, I'm here because my dad just passed away too. Well, three months ago, but it seems like yesterday. He left me this place and I'm just looking it over, trying to decide what to do with it."

"Oh Melanie, I didn't know. I'm sorry to barge in on you like this."

"No, no. It's fine. To be honest, I appreciate the company. It's a little spooky in here. So quiet."

"Well, how about I help you look the place over, see what condition it's in. I think you'll need to get the utilities turned back on for starters," Roger suggested.

"Yes I do, and I'd appreciate the help if you have time. I'm feeling a little, well...overwhelmed," I admitted.

"My pleasure. There's just one condition," he added and smiled sheepishly.

"What's that?"

"That you join me tomorrow for a picnic lunch at the tree fort."

I laughed and anxiously agreed.

I arrived a little past noon the next day and parked behind Roger's Jaguar. As I walked around the corner of the schoolhouse, I saw that he had been waiting for me, sitting in the middle of the old tree fort on a red and white checked tablecloth. He was leaning back against one of the tree trunks, sipping a glass of wine and looking out over the glistening water of the lake.

When he heard me approach, he turned, sat his glass down on top of a cooler, and then jumped up and ran across the playground to meet me—just as he had done so many times before, so long ago.

"You've gotta see this," he said excitedly, grabbing the apple tart I'd brought with one hand and pulling me toward the fort with the other."

"What?"

"It's so cool!"

I laughed at his youthful excitement.

"Look!" he said, pointing to a sturdy upper branch when we reached the base of the tree.

At first, I didn't see it. The vow was so faint, as though the old tree's bark had tried to erase it over the years, but then I saw the indentation of a heart with "RJ + MJ 4·ever" in the center.

"How sweet," I said. "I don't remember you carving that into the tree."

"Neither do I," he admitted. "I don't think I did. Must have been one of our friends," he said as he placed the pie on top of the cooler.

"Probably so," I agreed.

The picnic he had prepared for us that day was one of the most decadent meals I'd ever had, indoors or out. He had made delicious gourmet sandwiches: chicken salad with raisins and cinnamon in pita bread, and ham and Swiss with green olive tapenade on sourdough. For sides, he'd brought chopped veggies, seasoned crackers, and a fresh fruit salad that he served with a dollop of Greek yogurt on top.

He had also selected a nice sweet blush wine to accompany our lavish picnic, and even brought plastic champagne flutes to drink it out of. The apple tart that I had brought for dessert worked well to round out the meal.

We sat in the old tree fort talking for nearly two hours that day. Our conversation took twists and turns as we discussed everything from our jobs and the environment to favorite TV shows and how we both loved to cook. We even talked briefly about our former failed marriages and relationships—typically taboo subjects among strangers. And that's what we were really. We remembered so much about each other as children, each of us being the other's first love, but many years had passed since then. Now, we were weary strangers who shared a youthful past.

Since his divorce, Roger had become a successful architect and worked mainly out of his home. But affairs of the heart were another matter. He told me that the few serious relationships he'd had were mismatched and short lived. He had begun to think that he would spend the rest of his life alone. As the afternoon sun glistened on the water of the lake, I admitted that I'd come to the same conclusion, that finding a true soul mate in this lifetime had, thus far, proven impossible.

Eventually, we gathered our things and then walked around the school grounds. We tried to peek into the schoolhouse, but all of the windows were boarded up. The doors were locked as well. We were both excited to see inside, so I told Roger that I would look around the house for the key.

"Sounds great," he said. "Do you have any plans for this property, Melanie?"

"No, not really. I love it and would hate to sell it, but I have no idea what I'd do with it." I told him about Dad's vision for the place, and then about another thought that I'd had. "It would make a great building site. I imagine at least three homes could be built on this side of the lake, sort of in a semicircle. They could face the road with the lake in back. I should have the school torn down and sell off lots. And that's probably what I'll have to do to get the money I need to renovate the main house. Hate to though," I added, looking up at the brick and stone structure. "It holds so many good memories for me."

"Well actually, I'd like to buy it, if you would be willing to sell it to me," he said.

"Really?" I was amazed that he was interested in the property, but then remembered him saying that he had come up to the house yesterday to talk to Dad about it. "What would you do with it, Roger?"

"I'm getting tired of living in the city, Mel, and I've been thinking of downsizing for a while now...both in regard to my home and my business," he said, looking out over the old playground. "I've got sort of a semi-retirement plan, I guess you could say. I'd like a place in the country, and this would be a perfect spot—not in the city, but not too far from city conveniences, entertainment, and health care."

"It is pretty perfect, isn't it," I said.

He looked back at me and nodded. "I'd keep the old schoolhouse, maybe turn it into my office, or add on to it. Not sure yet, but I wouldn't tear it down, Mel." He smiled. "Too many good memories here for me too. But I'm interested in buying the entire property," he added quickly, "not just a lot. I'd pay a fair price for it, and I'm ready to buy as soon as you're ready to sell. So, you'd have plenty to fix up the house and could get started on it right away if you want."

"That sounds like a wonderful plan, Roger. But are you sure? Have you checked out other properties in the area?"

"Yes, I've been looking for a little while but haven't found anything that felt just right. Then yesterday, when I came to visit Mom, I passed by here and had an epiphany," he straightened and smiled broadly, like he was terribly proud of himself for having the revelation.

I laughed, seeing the boy in him once more. "Okay then. Let me talk to a local real estate agent and get it appraised, get some comps, and then we can go from there."

He nodded, still smiling broadly, and stuck his hand out to shake on it.

Over the next few weeks, I made loads of progress in cleaning out the house. Roger helped nearly every day. We got the utilities back on; sold, donated, or threw away a ton of stuff; and replaced the old carpet with hardwood flooring.

One Friday afternoon, I got a call from the real estate agent with an appraisal on the school property and was pleasantly surprised. It was much higher than I had expected. After ending the call, I was hesitant about giving Roger the news. I planned to think it over, to sleep on it, before deciding on an asking price.

Roger had been so helpful the past few weeks, and he was an old friend. I wanted to offer him a lower price than what the land appraised for, but enough to cover the bulk of my renovation costs, so I needed to think on just what that price should be.

"Was that the agent?" he asked, coming through the front door with an armload of cut wood to stack on the fireplace grate.

So much for my plan, I thought. "Where did you get the wood?"

"Fella next door. Nice old gent," he said as he placed the logs in the fireplace. "He was cutting down a small birch next to his house. Looked like he was struggling a bit, so I offered to help. He, in turn, offered us some firewood," he added, straightening up and beaming at me, proud of his bounty.

That's when it happened. That's when I knew I was falling in love with him. I don't know if it was because I was so physically tired, or so mentally stressed over design choices and what price to put on the school property, or what...but I started to cry. His smile instantly disappeared and he quickly came to me and wrapped me in his arms.

"Melanie, what's wrong?"

"Oh Roger, I have no idea what to ask for the school property. You've been so helpful, and I want to repay you for that. Give me some time to settle on a price, okay? Just a few days?"

"Ah Mel," he said soothingly, gently rocking me from side to side as I stood there in his arms. "Are you sure you even want to sell it? It's okay if you don't. It is, really. We'll do whatever you want with the place."

I pushed away from him and looked up into his face. "No, no! I want you to have it. I love what you have planned. I...I just want to give you a really good deal on it."

"Oh geeze, is that what you're worried about?" He laughed. "Well, I can take care of that. How about *I* offer *you* a price?" I just stared at him, blinking. He laughed again, so hard this time that he let go of me and bent over, his hands on his knees, tears coming to his own eyes. "That look," he managed, "it's hysterical, Mel!"

"Very funny," I said, scowling at him now.

He composed himself then. "Okay, okay. I'll offer twice what the place appraised for," he said, hands on his hips, looking me square in the eye, trying to be serious. It didn't work. I just stood there, dumbfounded and blinking at him again. He bent over double again with laughter.

"Roger Scott Jennings, you stop laughing at me," I said, feigning insult but about to start laughing myself because his reaction was so comical and his own laughter so infectious.

He stopped laughing and looked up, surprised. "You remembered my middle name!"

"Yes, of course," I said curtly.

He walked to me, beaming, and stuck out his hand, just as he had that day in front of the school. "Twice as much. Is it a deal?"

"Absolutely not!" I said, sincerely appalled. "I said I wanted to offer you a real deal on the place, not rob you!"

"Ah Mel, I've got plenty of dough. More than I know what to do with. I have no kids to spend it on, and my mom is being well taken care of. Sell me Mary's Elementary, Mel. Sell her to me and I promise to make her beautiful for you again. Now hurry up. Shake on it. There's the plumber pulling into the driveway," he said, looking up and out the front windows. He grabbed my right hand and gave it a good shake, then grabbed me by the

96

shoulders and kissed me quickly on the forehead. "There, even sealed with a kiss." He winked and turned to meet the plumber at the back door. I stood there stunned, staring as he hurried away. "Come on, Melanie Ann James! You need to tell him where you want the washer and dryer," he called back at me, chuckling.

Three weeks later, on a sunny Monday morning, we closed the deal on the school property and then had another picnic at the tree fort to celebrate. This time, I brought fried chicken, baked beans, and slaw. He brought the apple pie and a bottle of wine. We ate and laughed and talked and planned. It was the happiest I'd felt in a very long time.

"Wanna see inside the school?" he said. "I think it's time we tore off those old boards." He reached over and grabbed a crowbar, holding it up proudly.

I laughed. His boyish nature always tickled me. I reached into my pocket and pulled out the key I'd found. "Sure! I'm anxious to see inside the place again."

We removed some of the boards covering the windows to let in some light, and then unlocked the front door. It was surreal being back inside the old school. Everything looked and smelled just the same as I'd remembered it, except it too seemed much smaller now.

The windows were tall but filthy, and the floorboards were worn with years of little feet scuffling about. The long, green chalkboard still covered the back wall, the teacher's desk sat to the right of the board, and a few student desks still remained scattered about. Old books were strewn over the floor, and we took some time gathering them up and stacking them by the front door, making plans to look through them later.

We then walked to the back of the school. Roger pointed out some water damage on the ceiling, noting that the roof would need to be replaced. I walked to the chalkboard and saw that there were still pieces of chalk lying on the tray. I picked one up and wrote a little note on the board, hoping that Roger would find it later: "Welcome Home." When I replaced the chalk to the tray and turned, I noticed something gold lying beside an old eraser at the other end of the tray.

"Roger?"

"Yeah," he called back from the side of the room where he was checking out the rotting windowsill.

"Come look at this."

He walked over and I held up the two gold wedding bands. "I found them just lying here on the chalk tray," I said, handing them to him.

"How bizarre," he said slowly, looking them over. "They're obviously old and worn."

"Who on earth would have put them here?"

"I have absolutely no idea. Bizarre," he repeated and then laid them gently back on the chalk tray.

After our brief tour, we returned to the tree fort to gather our things. As we began cleaning up, Roger said, "You know, we fell in love right here when we were kids. I kissed you that day in this very spot, and that's all it took. I was hooked! Who knows what might have been if they hadn't closed this old place down and sent us off to different school districts."

"Hey, the way I remember it, *I* kissed *you* that day!" I insisted, acting boldly feminist, but not remembering which way it really happened.

He laughed boyishly and said, "Well then, it must be my turn."

Suddenly, without thinking of anything but the two of us being in that same special place where we had been together so long ago as children, he put his arms around me. I leaned toward him and we kissed. It was a long, passionate kiss this time. And then we kissed again. And again. And again.

Early the next day, I arrived back at my father's house, at my new old house, to meet with the building inspector. As he began climbing a ladder by the front door to check the roof, a delivery truck pulled into the drive. It was a local florist, and the driver soon walked up the front steps with an armload of three bouquets of roses: a dozen pink sweethearts; a dozen yellow; and eleven white roses surrounding a single, perfect red rose in the center. On the enclosed card, Roger had written a silly but sweet little poem to explain the symbolic bouquets:

A rose for each year of my life without you.
You were my childhood sweetheart.
You are once again my friend.
You must be an angel sent from Heaven,
Because you have made my heart beat again.

I had always thought that if any man was ever able to destroy the wall I'd built up after my last relationship ended so badly, it would take him a while. I imagined he'd have to do it a little at a time, the way my wall had been built. But it didn't happen that way at all. Instead, it came crashing down all at once. Or maybe there was a weak point, like my father's wooden doors in a structure of brick and steel.

In less than a year, Roger has turned the old schoolhouse into a beautiful place. He kept the main structure as a foyer with a library and guest bath on one side and a large office on the other where he can work and meet with clients. He added on to the back and built a modest bedroom, kitchen, and a full bath for himself—but designed it so that a second story could be added later if needed by future owners.

The side yard, which had been the playground, was now a lovely patio area bordered with lush landscaping. And just off the patio is a small, kidney-shaped pool with a rock waterfall at the far end.

He refurbished the stone cottage and then led me to it one day, making me promise to keep my eyes closed. When I opened them, there was a huge ribbon tied on the front door handle. He offered it to me to do with as I pleased, but suggested it would make a great little antique and gift shop. And that's just what I intend to do with it.

The old tree fort still stands at the edge of the lake. Roger has placed heavy wrought iron benches and tables on either side, making our occasional picnics much more comfortable affairs now.

At our last picnic, he showed me his newest discovery. On the tree trunk, below the heart with our initials in it, there are other initials carved in such tiny letters that they are barely noticeable: WJJ. He said they showed up again on the chalkboard one day, next to the "Welcome Home" message I'd left for him. But I had not written my mother's initials on the tree or on the chalkboard that day.

Meanwhile, I've completed the renovations on the home my father built. It's once again full of life and fresh air—a modernized version of my parent's original structure. I know they are happy with what I've done to the place. I sense their presence often.

Roger has sent me a dozen roses every month since we met, or met again, I should say. And with each bouquet, the ratio of white and red roses has changed. Another dozen arrived today: eleven red roses surrounding a single white rose in the center. The enclosed envelope contained no note this time—only a simple gold wedding band that once laid beside an old chalkboard, waiting to be found.

Dad, if you're still watching, it looks like it's going to be a wonderful new century. And Mom, thanks for your little messages. I got the hint, and I think Roger did too. Thanks to you both, we have a beautiful new estate.

A Bedtime Story

It was a crisp winter evening. The night sky was filled with stars. The full moon shone brightly on the glistening snow, the kind of snow that crunched when you walk on it.

Brian was snuggled up in his pajamas under his colorful Superman comforter, wide awake and waiting for his grandfather to come and tell him a bedtime story. While he waited, he looked around the room at all of his "stuff" to make sure his older brother hadn't taken anything without asking.

His bat and glove still stood in the corner, the rattlesnake skin was stretched across the top of his fish tank, and the kachina doll Uncle Ellis had given him last year for his birthday was still leaning against the dresser mirror. All of his best stuff was in its usual place. For once, Robby hadn't touched a thing.

He settled back, pulled the comforter up under his chin, and continued to wait patiently. He knew his grandfather would come. It was their Friday night ritual, and this was Friday night, his parent's "date night." All during the school week, Brian looked forward to spending this time with his grandfather, and especially to hearing what his next story would be. He never told the same story twice, and they were all true stories, no fairytales or fantasies. And Brian loved them all.

Takoda Hopewell was a very famous and well-respected man. He was also a busy man with many responsibilities, but he always spent time with his family, especially his favorite grandchild. Brian held great promise. He was a smart, inquisitive child already, at the young age of eight. Takoda hoped that he was still alive to see the boy turn into a young man, and that Brian would follow in his footsteps and become a leader, perhaps a better leader than he had been himself.

When Takoda came through his grandson's bedroom door, he smiled at him and then stood for a moment, looking around at the room. Brian watched him with big, unsleepy eyes. Neither said a word to the other. Both knew the routine. And both enjoyed it immensely.

Takoda moved around the spacious room, picking up an object or two and inspecting it, thinking, deciding on the theme of the evening's narrative. Once he had decided and was satisfied, he sat down in the big oak rocking chair that his daughter-in-law had placed in her son's room for him. He rocked gently for a moment, smiling down at Brian, who smiled back with bright, anticipating eyes. And then, Takoda began to tell him a bedtime story.

"It was the season of the eagle. Animals of every kind freely roamed the lush, green land. The great oaks, redwoods, and pines reached high toward the crystal blue sky. Fruits and berry bushes were plentiful. Lakes and rivers were full of fish, and springs brought forth clean, clear water.

"The man and his son had ceased their hunting in the forest and now lay on their bellies behind the fire bushes and vines, watching the shoreline and waiting. They breathed silently, their muscles alert but motionless. The father had taught his son well. To move, to attract attention, could sometimes mean death.

"A dozen or more emerged from the water. They had come from an enormous ship that remained out at sea, far from shore. The beings wore head coverings and heavy suits that seemed to restrict their movements. They bore metallic objects about their bodies that attracted the sun, and all carried long, dark sticks.

"They were grotesque, but did not look like vicious beasts, evil spirits, or the monsters of a dream. But they also did not look anything like the man and his son. And when the wind shifted, they could smell the foul odor of these beings. The two hunters were extremely cautious and filled with awe as they witnessed the arrival of aliens to their world.

"The man had heard stories about such beings with mysterious powers. Some claimed to have seen these beings themselves. There were even those who told of being captured by them, examined, and then returned safely. The man had never believed these tales, had laughed at those who told them. Now he believed.

"As the group on the shore began to move away in different directions, the father whispered a word to his son in a voice like the wind. They began to move back through the bush, still on their bellies, in a silent retreat. Finally, after reaching a safe distance where they could not be seen or heard by those on the shore, they stood again and ran back to warn the others.

"This began the season of the vulture. By the third long cycle, the land had begun to spoil. The dawn of the fourth brought swift decline. During the fifth, they attempted repairs, which were embraced by some, feared by others. The sixth cycle brought turmoil and chaos, and they turned to us for help once more, but almost too late. No eagle flew free. Much of the land was barren. The sky had turned from crystal blue to battle gray. Only a trickle of precious fresh water remained."

"Grandfather," Brian interrupted, "why didn't we make them leave? We could have, couldn't we? There were many more of us then. We could have sent them back to the sea. They would have been very afraid and others would not have come. The season of the eagle would have remained forever."

"Shoshoni," Takoda said, preferring to call his grandson by his middle name, "we believed them when they said they meant us no harm, that they came in peace, and that they were only explorers from a far off land."

"That was a mistake, Grandfather."

"Yes."

"But we fixed it, didn't we?"

"Yes. Time passed and they began to see."

"They were wise and turned to us for help."

"Yes. Clean water now flows. The sickness is leaving the land. The great eagle soars once more, and the skies above our ancestor's homelands have returned to blue."

"Tell me that story now, Grandfather! How did we save our world? How did you become President and Chief?"

Takoda smiled at his grandson. "Those are bedtime stories for other nights, Shoshoni, but I will tell you all of them. And you must remember and pass them on. You must help to keep the season of the eagle for many long cycles to come.

The Lore

Back Then:

It had to have been the coldest, wettest May in Kentucky's history. There had been three solid weeks of some sort of precipitation, and by the end of the third week, everyone was pretty much in a foul mood. If it wasn't actually raining, it was drizzling or misting, and if it wasn't doing either one of those, it was so damn muggy that the humidity was ninety-nine percent, so it might as well have been raining. The farmers who had already planted crops lost them all and had to replant when the soggy soil dried out some.

Along with the unusual moisture that insisted on hanging around, there were some really frigid temps. I remember Gramps saying that there was even frost out on the fields two mornings that particular May. The news hadn't said anything about the frost, and I didn't see it for myself, but I can't imagine Gramps fibbing about it. Fibbing just wasn't Gramps' style. So as far as I'm concerned, it's a definite fact there was a frost in Kentucky in May of 1975. And as far as I'm concerned, Gramps was right about the leprechauns too.

When It Started:

I spent what seemed an eternity at Smither's Public Library doing research for an oral report that May. It was for our final exam in "Ms." (God forbid Miss or Mrs.) Brenner's eighth grade Social Studies class. Our assignment was to answer the question: "Why is there no industry in Muddy Creak?" Yeah, that's right, Muddy *Creak*, like the sound a rusty hinge makes. Gramps said "some old illiterate settler son of a bitch" probably named the place and nobody since has had the heart to change it. They should have, if you ask me. Who'd want that joke on their business card, you know?

I couldn't come up with any other valid reason why the town didn't have even one factory of any kind. The Creak is less than twenty miles away from two larger cities, and according to *The Herald*, it's always been accessible, since the old railroad tracks run all the way to the river where the locks are. There's plenty of available land here still today, and there's always been ample power and sewer facilities for industry.

So, I took a chance and did my report on the misspelled name hypothesis. Believe it or not, I got an "A"—the only one I ever got in Ms. Brenner's class. Jenny's theory, which got her a big fat "C," as I remember, was probably a lot closer to the truth, though. I still remember how she started her report: "Why Muddy Creak Has No Industry, by Jennifer Ann Biggs. I believe the reason there are no factories in Muddy Creak is because the whole town has a curse on it."

I'd noticed it too—all the weird things that had happened over the years. Around the third day at the library, my eyes were getting tired of looking for the same key words about industry in the newspaper headlines on the library's new microfiche machine. So around noon, I thought about quitting and going back home to have lunch with Gramps. He'd been peeling apples from his small orchard when I left. "Come on back and get you some of these fried pies 'bout noon, Timmy. Studyin's good and all, but too much is bound to turn your brain to mush!" he had yelled as I was going out the door that morning. But just when I reached up to turn off the machine, I noticed the article about the Middleton baby:

**Six Month Old Daughter
of Sam and Tammy Middleton
Found Dead at Proposed Industrial Site**

The article stated that the baby was found hanging upside down from a tree, its legs tied to a low branch. Directly beneath the child was a large, black cauldron filled with some sort of green, sticky muck. The last line read: "Who is doing these horrible things?"

Up until then, I wasn't too sure about Gramps' leprechaun story myself, but after I read that article, I started looking for others that mentioned strange things that had happened in Muddy Creak. And I found them too, plenty of them. I just wasn't stupid enough to write my report on it like Jenny had.

In the News:

I spent most of my summer vacation that year in the library, and I came up with over a hundred strange events that had happened in our small, rural town from the first printing of *The Herald* in 1898 up to that summer in '75. Several articles reported chickens being covered in sticky goo and stuck to the backs of pigs or horses, hundreds of tiny holes cut in the sides or roofs of barns and sheds, and fields of corn stalks being woven together. In each case, either a strange gold coin or some unidentifiable green substance was found at the scene. Others mentioned bizarre things that were found tied to the train tracks—such as a live Arctic reindeer and fifty-five washing machines.

There were also reports of at least thirty-five suspicious deaths. In addition to Mr. and Mrs. Middleton's baby, there were nine kids, seventeen old folks, and eight others of various ages who died from "unknown causes," or under "strange circumstances." The eight others were the most bizarre.

In May of 1938, the decapitated remains of two twelve year-old boys were found at the old Gray's Hill cemetery. The paper said that two elderly women stumbled upon the bodies, literally, while visiting their husbands' graves on Memorial Day. One of the women stated that, "Their heads were cut clean off and stuck up on top of two headstones." On the chest of each headless victim was a single, large gold coin. There were no markings on the coins except three symbols on one side that no one was able to decipher. There wasn't much of an investigation, according to the paper, and no one was ever convicted of the crime.

Earlier that same year, a sixteen year-old girl was found wandering along the side of US 23, not far from Gray's Hill, with hardly enough blood in her to keep her alive. She was taken to the hospital in nearby Taylorsville, and then transferred to the mental asylum in Lexington six weeks later. She only spoke once after they found her. And what she said was just a single word: "green."

One George W. Bowman, a childless widower from Arkansas, was visiting his old army buddy,

Lester Peterson, on Thanksgiving in 1958 when his car exploded while he was backing out of Lester's driveway. According to Mr. Peterson, "George was the nicest guy in the world." He told the detective on the case that he didn't believe his friend had even one enemy. Despite the fact that the investigators could find no reason for the car to explode, George Bowman's death was ruled an accident.

The next month, a former resident of Muddy Creak, Emma Riverton, was visiting her sister, Wynona, over the holidays one winter. Wynona found her floating face down in the bathtub on Christmas morning. Old Doc Riley, who wasn't really all that old back then, said it wasn't a heart attack or any other natural cause of death. So, they called it a suicide, despite Wynona's insistence that her sister would never commit such a sin. Apparently, she was also upset about where her sister could have gotten the green bubble bath she was soaking in.

Another woman choked on chicken noodle soup, of all things, while visiting her daughter, Becky Smith, who lived on Black Fork Road on the outskirts of Muddy Creak. They were sitting at the dining room table eating dinner on a Friday night. After putting a spoonful of soup in her mouth, Becky's mother looked out the window and began to choke. Becky told reporters that when she tried to help, her mother kept pointing out the window and acting like she was scared to death. But Becky couldn't see anything in the back yard except her prize-winning rose bush, right where it had always been.

Two other victims simply disappeared. One was a man in his forties who supposedly "ran away from home," leaving his wife and four children to wonder what had happened to him. He has never been found. The other was a seventeen year-old senior at Taylorsville High. Her parents, classmates, and fellow cheerleaders could think of no reason for her to abruptly leave town. She was a straight "A" student, got along with her parents and siblings, and had a boyfriend that "she adored." However, some speculated that she "could have been pregnant" and left town because of this shame. Still, she had never returned, with or without a baby in tow.

There were only two things I could see that tied any of these events together. First, more often than not, either a gold coin or a mysterious green substance was found at the scene of the crime. Second, the strange occurrences seemed to happen about every twenty years—just enough time in between for people to forget.

Gramps' Story:

That fall, I helped Gramps pick several bushels of apples and load them, along with two cases of his homemade cider, into the back of his old '55 Chevy half-ton pickup. Then we headed to town to sell them to Joe Mackie, who owned a dry goods store that had a vegetable stand out front stocked with locally grown produce.

After we unloaded and Joe paid Gramps for the delivery, we bought a hunk of bologna and some crackers and joined a couple of other local farmers who were sitting by an old wood stove in the back of the store. The weather had turned cool quickly that year, and the warmth of the stove was a welcome respite after our long day's work. Gramps pulled up an old ladder-back chair, I sat on a wooden milk crate, and we joined in their conversation. Well, Gramps joined in, big time as it turned out, and I mostly just listened.

The men were talking about all of the weird things that had been going on in the town. Old Ace, who died of a stroke or something about a week later, was telling about one of his cows foaming at the mouth and the vet not being able to find anything wrong with it. He said the foam was "green as grass."

They all had some story to tell, but Gramps' was the best. He'd been sitting there just listening for quite a while, eating his bologna and crackers. Then he got up, got a pickled egg out of the jar in the meat cooler, and told them he knew exactly what was going on in The Creak. He said we had some little visitors in town, and that they all had better "watch their p's and q's."

"What the Sam Hill are you talking about, Caleb?" asked Tom Tackett, who was perhaps the wealthiest farmer and largest land owner in the county.

"Look, I ain't said nothin' to nobody about this before because I knew the whole town would think I was loony. But you boys know me, don't you? And you know I ain't one to go spinnin' no yarns, right?" The men looked at Gramps and nodded. "Well, I'm gonna tell you what I saw, but I don't want a damn one of you laughin' when I tell it, ya hear?"

"Well, go on, Caleb. What did you see?" asked Old Ace, who still seemed a bit agitated about his foaming cow.

Gramps nodded, but didn't say anything for another few seconds. Maybe he was thinking of how to start his story, or whether to tell it at all. But then he spoke, and I stopped eating my bologna.

"You all remember the old Mays homestead out back of my place, don't you? You remember what it looks like?" Gramps asked.

"Hell, Caleb, I ain't been out there since we were kids," said Tom.

"Well, it's pretty much gone now, nothin' left but the stone foundation and part of the back wall. And it's all grown up with Kudzu, Honeysuckle and Sweet Gum trees. But you can still see one window in the back wall pretty good. There's no glass in it anymore, though."

"Yeah, that's right," Old Ace agreed. "I was up there lookin' for Lula Belle just the other day. She got out again, and I swear I can't find a hole in the fence anywhere. Don't know how that damn cow's getting' out." He paused when the others snickered, not about Lula Belle getting loose, but about Old Ace's wife naming their cows, every last one of them. "I'm not ashamed to say that old place still gives me the jitters," he added, ignoring his friends' laughter.

"Ace, you old fool, that place ain't haunted," Tom insisted. "That was just a bunch of bull my pappy got started to scare us back then. Now go on, Caleb. Tell it already. I gotta get back to work," he added, and then began to pull on the long, gray hairs of his right eyebrow.

"Okay, well, I was out squirrel huntin' last week. It was on Sunday afternoon. And when I got pretty close to the old Mays place, I saw something dartin' around in the bushes. I figured it was a deer, but the way the weeds were movin' was a bit odd. So, I kept my eye steady on the place as I was goin' past it, and when I got right in front, I heard a queer noise. I looked up real quick and saw somebody sitting in that window, sort of half in and half out. The minute I spotted him, he spotted me too, and he jumped out the window and was gone like a flash. I hollered: 'Hello there,' because I thought it was a kid or somethin', but there was no answer. So, I started walkin' all about the place, lookin' for him, but I got to thinkin' about what he looked like, and I don't mind tellin' you boys that I got a little buggy, so I high-tailed it outta there."

"Seems to me I remember my daddy telling me about seeing something like that one time," said Joe as he walked up and leaned on the meat cooler, folding his arms over his considerable belly.

"What was so funny about how he looked? You don't think it was a kid?" Old Ace asked.

"Nope, not after I really thought about it. Ya see, he was green, from head to toe. At first, I thought it was paint or somethin', just some kids playing army and camouflaged themselves or somethin' like that. But I'm not sure. He was dressed funny and real little, no more than three feet tall if he'd been standing up. And I didn't hear or see any other kids out there that day. What would such a young kid be doin' way out there by himself?"

"Did he have pointed shoes, Caleb?" Tom asked loudly, slapping his knee. "Maybe what you got yourself a glimpse of was an elf!" With that, Tom started to laugh and dropped the plug of chewing tobacco he'd fished out of the pouch onto the top of the wood stove.

"Yep, or a little green man from Mars," Joe added, laughing at Tom trying to retrieve his chewing tobacco without burning his fingers as much as he was at Gramps' story.

"I figured as much, you old jackasses!" Gramps roared as he quickly stood up. "I reckon it'll be all around town that I'm some crazy old fool now."

The gossip started the next day, of course. And as it turned out, the story going around was that Gramps was "losin' his marbles" and "seeing little green men," just as he predicted. But I believed him, every word, because it had been about twenty years since the last strange events I'd read about in the newspaper articles.

April, 1995:

I own *The Herald* now. I bought it from Charlie's wife after he passed away about ten years ago. I always thought I'd leave The Creak one day for the big city and make my fortune, but I never did. Instead, I ended up marrying Jenny Biggs and we've got three kids now.

Billy, our oldest, came home from school this afternoon and told about a kid who fainted in Art class while they were making decorations for St. Patrick's Day. The kid was just setting there staring at the construction paper when he fainted and fell out of his chair. That's the third weird thing that's happened lately. Last week, they found an old boat down by the river that was covered in thick, green moss. And Doc Smith, the town vet, is missing.

It's been twenty years, and I've been waiting. It's time. I'll sit down with Jenny and the boys tonight, set some ground rules. No one goes out alone until this is over. Tomorrow, I'll share my research findings with the mayor and the sheriff. I just pray they believe me, that they realize the danger and warn the citizens of Muddy Creak, maybe set a curfew and do some night patrols. How can they not believe me? I have historical evidence of the twenty year cycle.

Then I'll go down to the Mini Mart and see if anyone's heard about any other strange events. Joe's son, Junior, took over his dad's dry goods store and turned it into a Mini Mart about the time I bought *The Herald*. There's always a bunch of regulars sitting around drinking coffee and bullshitting, just like in the old days. Some things never change. I'll try to get some of the guys together for a hunting trip. With a little luck, we'll get some photographic evidence. And with a lot of luck, we might even catch us one of those little green bastards before they kill somebody this time.

I think I'll see if Billy wants to come along. I just might have to tell them Gramps' leprechaun story, and he might as well hear it firsthand. Some of them might even remember hearing about it when they were kids. And some of them might just believe the lore. Stranger things have happened.

Re-creation

Josephine pulled up in the carport just as Louise was fetching the tackle box from the screened-in back porch. The modified tackle box had been the perfect organizer for her watercolors. When she heard the sound of the Jeep's engine, she groaned, grabbed a zipper pouch with her spare brushes, and returned to the living room.

"Oh Jo, did you *have* to drive that thing today? It doesn't even have any doors on it for goodness sakes," she said as Josephine came in the front door.

"If you're so particular about how you get somewhere, Lucky Lou, you should have learned how to drive yourself!" Josephine grabbed the easel that was propped by the door, took it out to the Jeep, and wedged it behind the seats. "Now come on, get in and stop your complaining. They made these seat belts here just to keep crabby old ladies like you from flying out."

Josephine was only five minutes younger than her twin sister but had teased her about being old for years. She'd also given her the nickname Lucky Lou when they were in their twenties. It seemed, at least to Josephine, that everything her sister did was golden. She was a straight "A" student and Homecoming Queen in high school. She'd married Leonard, who had a stable job, a great personality, and treated Louise like a princess. And, she'd gone to college on a full scholarship. A few years after graduating, she began gaining success and a bit of fame as an artist. Josephine had not been so lucky.

"Will you ever stop calling me that?"

"Not likely," Josephine said with a smile.

"Well, the paper said sunset would be at 7:45 this evening, and it's only 5:00 now, so you can drive slow. We've got plenty of time to get to Elkhorn and get set up," Louise reasoned as she reluctantly climbed into the passenger seat and buckled up.

"Oh, it only takes about fifteen minutes to get there from here."

"Drive *slow*," Louise reminded her. "How did you say you found out about this beautiful spot?"

"I told you the other day on the phone, remember? Harry and I went camping up there a couple of weeks ago."

Louise's increasing forgetfulness was concerning Josephine. Sixty seemed way too young to be getting senile, but she wasn't sure at what age early onset Alzheimer's might strike. And she worried that if Louise got the dreaded disease, which had become the plague of their generation, she was apt to get it too.

"Oh, that's right, I remember you telling me about it now," Louise said absently.

"The sunset from up there was absolutely a Heavenly sight. It'll be the best sketches you've ever done, I promise. Did you get your easel fixed?"

"Yep, yesterday. I went with Mary Sue. She's the sweetest thing. A person couldn't ask for a better neighbor. She had to take Eddy to the Orthodontist and get his braces fixed. You know one of those wires in Eddy's mouth broke and stuck right into the side of his cheek! Lordy, I wouldn't want those things in my mouth."

"Me either," Josephine agreed.

"Oh, and we stopped by the grocery, so I got the ingredients for the side dishes. All you'll have to bring to the family reunion next week is the ham. I told Ola you'd bring the ham, since I knew you could buy one already baked."

"Well I'm glad of that. I never was any count at cookin'. Too tedious and time-consuming, if you ask me."

Josephine had always hated to cook, or wash dishes for that matter. When they were kids, she would help her father mow the lawn and tend to the garden while Josephine helped her mother with the housework and kitchen duties. The arrangement suited both sisters quite nicely.

Louise hated to touch the fuzzy green worms their father made them pick off the tomato plants, but Josephine didn't mind them at all. She would pinch them off the vines and mash them in two, bare-handed.

"Eva Marie called yesterday," Louise said. "She probably won't come to the reunion. She's afraid the heat will get to her, or that she'll go into labor. The poor thing's two weeks overdue."

Eva Marie was their niece, their younger brother's daughter. Her mother had died when she was just a toddler, so Donny had asked his sisters if they would help him take care of her. Donny was a salesman and traveled quite a bit, often staying away from home for several days at a time. As it turned out, neither sister had children of their own. They adored Eva Marie and were happy to share the responsibility of helping to raise her.

"Lord have mercy, I imagine being pregnant is bad enough, let alone having to suffer with a child being overdue," Josephine said.

"By the way, when did you start seeing this Harry? You gonna bring him to the reunion?"

"No! I am certainly *not* bringing him to the reunion. I'm not going to introduce him to the family until I'm sure I like him," Josephine said, rather irritated.

"Like him? I thought you said you went camping with him."

"I did."

"Well, what did you do, sleep in separate tents?"

"Lou, you slay me. No, we didn't sleep in separate tents; we slept together."

Josephine could tell her sister didn't approve of her relationship with Harry, but she refused to apologize about her lifestyle.

"Aren't you afraid to camp out like that in nothing but a flimsy tent that snakes could crawl into?"

"Louise, snakes can't get in; there's a zipper."

"Well, doesn't lying on that hard, damp ground hurt your arthritis?"

"Yes, but so does getting out of bed every morning, and I'm not ready to give in to Old Arthur just yet. And we use these comfy mats under our sleeping bag. Besides, the exercise does my arthritis good. You need to exercise more. It keeps the body limber and your mind sharp. You've always been such a scaredy cat, Lucky Lou. If it wasn't for me dragging you out of that depressing old house of yours, I don't think you'd get out at all. If you were more active, you'd feel better."

"My house isn't depressing," Louise said, defensively.

"It is so. All you ever do is sit around and think about Leonard. He's dead, Lou. Been dead many a year. It's time you moved on with your life. Find you another good man."

"Josephine! I can't believe you'd say a thing like that. You just don't forget somebody you spent more than thirty years with!"

"Well, I wouldn't know. Just the thought of spending thirty years with the same man makes me a little queasy. And don't call me *Josephine.* You know I hate it."

"Leonard was a good man. And I'd rather be married to the same man and have some security and stability in my life instead of gallivanting all over the country with every Tom, Dick...or *Harry* like you've done. And what have you got to show for it?"

"What do you mean? I've got *two* homes and *two* cars, and they're all paid for. On top of that, I've still got a fair nest egg for retirement. And I never had to put up with somebody belittling me, or slapping me around, or accusing me of cheating on him just because he thought I'd stayed a little too long at the grocery store!"

"I know, Jo. You've never had much luck with the fellas. Oh please slow down around these curves. This doorless buggy gives me the jitters."

"Well, we're almost there," Josephine said as she eased off of the accelerator a bit. "And don't think you've gotten me off the topic of you getting out of that house and finding you another fella, either."

"Ha! Jo, you're a hoot!"

"You're right, Leonard was a saint, but you can't deny that he was a little stingy. If you wanted anything, even a pair of new shoes, you had to ask his permission. And why? Because it was *his* money, right? He was the breadwinner. Well, not me. It'd be a cold day in hell before I'd ever ask *my* husband if I could buy a pair of shoes. You just went from one daddy to another, Louise."

"I know, Jo, I know. You and I are different. But I knew Leonard was tight with his money because he was saving for our old age. And now I've got plenty of money and don't have to worry about a thing, thanks to him being *stingy*. I know what you mean, though. Somehow that doesn't quite make up for that pair of pink summer sandals I wanted that time we went shopping in Nashville. They had little silver stars on the toes and laces that tied up around your ankle, remember?"

"Oh Lou, I love you, you know that?" Josephine asked, regretting that she had argued with her sister.

"Yes, I know. Love you too. And I'm glad you're my...

Louise didn't get to finish her sentence, but Josephine knew what she was going to say. Had there been time to answer, she would have said that she was glad Louise was her sister too.

The Jeep rolled about six times after its right rear tire hit the soft shoulder of the newly repaved road just before they got to the entrance of the campground. It finally came to rest on its passenger's side in the middle of a field recently sown with dogwood saplings.

Louise's seat belt hadn't held, and she was thrown several feet in the air. The force of her body reconnecting with the earth had broken her back. Josephine was still in the Jeep when it stopped rolling. The ambulance drivers would discover later that her skull had been cracked in three places and both of her legs were completely crushed. Her last thought as she lay with her head against the cool ground, peering out through the broken windshield, was a prayer. She prayed that Louise was watching the sun set over the top of the mountain.

Yes Jo, I see it, Louise thought. *Just beyond that little sapling. And it is a Heavenly sight, just like you said.*

The bright glare of the delivery room made it hard for Marcus to hide his tears. It was horrible for him to see his wife in so much pain. Eva Marie had insisted on a natural childbirth but was now seriously regretting her decision. They had worried there might be complications, but so far, everything seemed to be going smoothly with the delivery.

As the baby crowned, Marcus looked at the top of his child's head with its fine, dark hair and wondered if it looked like it belonged to a boy or a girl. They had decided that they didn't want to know the sex of the baby ahead of time, but now the anticipation was maddening.

As Marcus tightly held her hand, Eva Marie gave birth to a pristine baby girl that sunny day in June. They named her Thea.

The following afternoon, Eva Marie walked slowly to the nursery window and looked down at the new person she had helped create. She was an emotional wreck, both incredibly happy and terribly sad at the same time.

Her arms were folded beneath her painfully full breasts as she attempted to console herself. Although she realized some must die as others are born, the logic did not ease the grief from the loss of her beloved aunts. She thought of how very different the women had been, yet how much each had taught her.

She never knew her own mother, but it was as if she'd had two other mothers her whole life, and both had just died at the same time. In a way, it was a bit of comfort knowing that they left the world together, just as they had arrived.

Standing at the window staring down at her newborn and waiting for feeding time, Eva Marie recalled cherished moments she'd spent with her aunts. Louise had taught her their family's secret recipe for carrot cake on her thirteenth birthday. She had written it down on a recipe card, which had a plastic cover and purple ribbon along its top edge. Eva Marie was so proud. It seemed to represent a rite-of-passage, her coming of age.

She remembered the time Josephine took her to the bank and opened a savings account for her when she was ten. Her father had been a little upset with his sister when he found out. But her Aunt Jo had just smiled, winked, and kissed his nose before riding off on the back of her latest boyfriend's Harley.

Eva Marie laughed out loud standing in the hospital corridor, even though salty tears were falling down her cheeks, when she remembered the time her aunts tried to sneak her graduation present into the garage late one night. Josephine had stopped the car and turned off the engine a couple of houses down the street. They were afraid that driving into the garage might wake her, since her bedroom was on the same side of the house as the driveway, and they wanted it to be a surprise waiting for her the next morning. So, they push the Mustang down the street, but had trouble pushing it up the slight incline of the driveway. They only made it about half way.

Her father had been up late that night doing paper work, and she was still awake in her room writing a final paper for her History class. They both heard a commotion outside, and Eva Marie rushed downstairs to find her father staring out of the window in the den, laughing so hard he couldn't catch his breath. She rushed over and looked out just in time to see her Aunt Lou running backwards behind the Mustang with her hands still on the trunk lid. Both the car and

Louise zoomed back down their driveway and up into the widow Robinson's front yard across the street, mowing down her prize azalea bush in the process.

As Eva Marie was reliving fond memories of Josephine and Louise, the two infants in bassinets on either side of Thea began to wail. She waited, but no nurse came to tend to them. She began to get angry as she looked around for someone, thinking of how horrible it would be for Thea to be crying so hard and no one coming to comfort her. But at present, her daughter was lying between these screaming babies looking incredibly peaceful and calm.

Then, she witnessed a peculiar thing. Thea looked directly into her mother's eyes, smiled, and turned her head to the screaming infant on her left and cooed. Within seconds, the neighboring child's crying subsided and she fell into a peaceful sleep. Thea then turned to the infant on her right and began making the same cooing noises. He too stopped crying.

Eva Marie stood transfixed. She wondered about the magical, unexplainable events that sometimes occurred, trying to decide if they happened simply by chance or held some divine purpose. With that thought, Eva Marie suddenly remembered the strange pact she overheard her aunts make one summer day years earlier.

The three were having a picnic at Josephine's cabin, and for once, the sisters had not argued during the entire outing. For desert, Louise had brought a watermelon, and she let Eva Marie use the butcher knife to cut the huge green fruit into two pulpy crimson halves. Then she cut the halves in two again, lengthwise, and they each took a section and ate the melon right out of the rind, giggling as its juice dribbled down their chins.

When they were cleaning up, Josephine told her sister about an obituary she had read in the newspaper the day before. A close friend of theirs from high school had died suddenly. They made plans to attend their former classmate's funeral, and then Josephine asked if either Louise or Eva Marie believed in ghosts. After a brief conversation on the topic, the sisters agreed that the one who died first would attempt to contact the other from the afterlife. Eva Marie had told them they were "morbid and nuts," and to not even think about trying to contact her. She said that she would probably have a heart attack and be dead right along with them if they did. Now, however, she almost wished they would try to contact her.

Eva Marie turned away from the nursery window and slowly walked back to her room to rest. After the evening feeding, she would shower and pack their things. Marcus would be there to take them home in the morning, and she could hardly wait to settle into a routine with Thea. That evening, Eva Marie got the last really good night's sleep that she would get for some time. She slept soundly, and on her stomach once more, the entire night.

On the Easter Sunday following Thea's tenth birthday, all of the family gathered at Marcus and Eva Marie's for dinner and a massive Easter egg hunt. Each person brought a dozen decorated eggs, and Marcus bought brightly colored plastic eggs to fill with surprise gifts.

He and Thea had stayed up until midnight the evening before thinking up the surprises to put in the plastic eggs. They filled some with a little strip of paper, like the ones that come in fortune cookies, with an I.O.U. written on it. One I.O.U read, *Don't have to do any chores for a whole week.* Another read, *Can stay up one hour past your bedtime.* They filled others with things like folded dollar bills, coins, and candy of all sorts. In one, Marcus placed a pair of tickets to a Tennessee Volunteer's game, hoping that his brother, Rob, would find it.

After the egg hunt, a lot of exchanging of plastic Easter eggs took place. Rob ended up paying his daughter, Jessie, twenty dollars for the one with the tickets in it. Eva Marie found the one with the I.O.U. that promised an extended bedtime. When she cracked open the egg and read its message, she ran over to Marcus, showed it to him and winked. He, in turn, chased his wife around the gigantic snowball bush in the corner of their front yard. By the time Eva Marie let him catch her, they were both covered in small white petals.

When dinner and the egg hunt were over, all of the women gathered in the kitchen while the men watched a game on television in the family room. This separation of the sexes during holiday gatherings had been a family tradition since their ancestors settled in Tennessee, according to Thea's Grandma Smith. Eva Marie told her daughter that it had something to do with bonding. Although the other kids were playing board games or video games in the upstairs playroom, Thea had joined the women's conversation in the kitchen.

"Don't you want to go play with the rest of the kids, sugar?" Grandma Smith asked.

"Not really," she said, and smiled. "I'll go up later, but I'd rather sit and talk with you all right now."

"Thea honey, you look just like your Great-aunt Jo when you smile," Grandma Smith said.

"She does, doesn't she?" Eva Marie agreed. "And I think she's gonna be just as good a cook as Aunt Louise was. Yesterday, she asked if she could bake that carrot cake you're eating all by herself. So I let her. What do you think? It tastes just like Aunt Lou's, if you ask me!"

"Why, it sure does! And I'm not just saying that because you're sitting right there either, Thea. This is every bit as good as Lou's! I just figured your momma baked it."

"Well, I didn't so much as sift the flour or break an egg," Eva Marie insisted. "I *was* in the kitchen the whole time, doing this and that. But Thea never asked me one single thing. She just looked at the recipe for a second and then put it back in the recipe box. I started to remind her that she'd need it to refer back to, but I figured she'd find that out for herself."

"But I didn't have to do that with this recipe, Momma," Thea said.

"You didn't? Well, you don't have a photographic memory, now do you?" Eva Marie teased.

"Nope, I just know that one."

"Well how odd," remarked Grandma Smith, as she stared at Josephine's dimples sunk into the sides of Thea's rosy cheeks.

Thea was up in her bedroom trying to whittle down the pile on her bed to only the items she felt she absolutely had to take with her to Berkeley when her mother called to her.

"Gramps is here, Thea!"

"Be down in a second."

Donny had come to see his granddaughter one last time before she left for college, and Eva Marie was still trying to ease her father's fears.

"Dad, she's old enough to make her own decisions. I'm not crazy about her going to school so far away either, but she's a smart, sensible young woman. She'll be fine. And no, I don't think she'll run off and get married on us. She says she doesn't believe in the "societal norms regarding the institution of marriage," but does believe in a "mature commitment" between two people. Here she comes, now stop worrying! She'll be fine."

"Hi, Gramps, how's it going?" Thea said as she bounded down the stairs.

"Great, Sweetie. Did you get my text message?" he asked, giving her a big hug.

"Yes, and I still can't believe it. Why did they leave all of that money to me? They didn't even know me, Gramps. You all told me they died the day before I was born. And why did you all wait until now to tell me about this?"

"I guess they just wanted you to have it, Thea. And we didn't tell you because we figured it would make the ultimate present, one that had been growing right along with you all these years. Both of their wills stipulated that the inheritance wasn't to be transferred until you reached legal age. They set it up like a trust fund. Pretty smart, those two were. You are now worth a small fortune, my dear."

"That was just so kind of them. And I can't even thank them. It's just still hard to believe. School will be paid for, I won't have to work part-time, and Mom and Dad won't have to take out a second mortgage just to pay for my education!" Thea laughed, thankful that those burdens had been lifted from her shoulders by two women she had never even known.

"Are you sure this is what you want to do, Sweetie? It seems that this going to be an awfully demanding curriculum."

"Yes, I'm sure. Engineering and Agriculture is the perfect double major for me. I hope to start up an epic organic foods business one day. Dad said he'd help with the bookkeeping. Mom's going to help with design and layout. I thought maybe you could help me with marketing? It'll be a family operation!" she said excitedly.

"That does sound pretty epic," Donny agreed, laughing at his granddaughter's enthusiasm. Of course I'll help. Do you think you'll still find time to paint?"

"Absolutely! It's my hobby, one I can actually make money with! I don't think I'll ever stop painting. It keeps me sane!" she said.

Eva Marie sat in the family room listening as Thea and her father talked in the kitchen. She smiled at Thea trying to ease her grandfather's fears and glanced up at the painting above the fireplace mantle. A New York gallery had commissioned Thea to paint several more like it. And Eva Marie agreed with the gallery's director; she had never seen a more beautiful sunrise.

The Fish Market

The elderly owner of a grocery and fish market was putting fresh Louisiana crawfish in an ice packed display bin one day when he spotted a disheveled, middle-aged man attempting to steal a loaf of freshly made sourdough bread.

He said to the man, "Excuse me, sir, you have to pay for that bread!"

The homeless man, startled that he'd been caught, jerked around to face the market owner, the loaf of bread still in his hand.

"I'm…I'm so sorry, but I don't have the money to pay for it. I have nothing, and I am so hungry," he said. He hung his head in shame, but then straightened and looked up again, trying to regain what little remained of his dignity. "Would you, by any chance, have some odd jobs that I might do to pay for my meal?"

The market owner felt sorry for the vagrant, but said, "Sir, it is only $2.12 for the bread. Do you not have even that much money on you?"

"I don't have a penny. I really am very sorry. But I haven't eaten in three days. Normally, I would never think of stealing...have never stolen anything in my whole life. But I lost my job a few months ago and haven't been able to find work. I have no relatives in these parts. I've been living on the streets, and I am just so hungry," he repeated.

Reluctantly, he handed the loaf of bread back as tears began to glisten in his eyes. The market owner could see that the man was at the end of his rope and thought of how awful it would be to be in the man's position.

The vagrant began backing up slowly, back toward the door, when he bumped into a display of newly stocked apples. One tumbled from the display, fell to the floor, and rolled to the toe of his ragged boot. An idea came to him and he quickly looked up with hope in his eyes.

"May I have this apple that has fallen? It is surely bruised now. And would you perhaps have any old, stale bread that you have thrown out? Any out of date canned foods you have put in the garbage, or any wilted vegetables that I might have?" he asked, excited about his brainstorm and speaking quickly.

The market owner smiled at the homeless man and asked, "What's your name, sir?"

The man blinked, taken aback by this simple question that no one had asked him for a long time. "My...my name is Kenneth...Ken Roberts," he replied.

"Well, I'm Raymond...Ray Anderson," the market owner said with a chuckle. He then laid the loaf of bread down on top of a crate of bananas, wiped his right hand onto his white apron, and stuck it out to his new acquaintance.

Kenneth hesitated for a second, looking down at the man's hand, and then quickly stuck out his own and shook to formalize the introductions.

"And what was your profession when you were gainfully employed, Mr. Roberts?"

"I...I was a farmer," Kenneth said, and then shook his head and began laughing and crying at the same time, considering the irony of his situation.

The market owner laughed heartily with him. "Well, Mr. Roberts, please do take the apple," he said as he bent, picked up the fallen fruit, and handed it to Kenneth. "Keep this loaf of fresh bread as well," he added, turning to retrieve the loaf and handing it to him.

"Thank you so much, sir. I...I don't know how to thank you."

"Come on back tomorrow morning at 8:00 a.m. sharp."

Kenneth looked earnestly at the man. "8:00 a.m., sir?"

"Yep. I'm getting tired, Ken, tired and old. My only son moved off up north last year, you see. Said he wasn't interested in taking over and running this 'damn little fish market in this damn little gator infested, podunk town.'" The man chuckled and shook his head, but looked back at Kenneth with sad eyes. "So, well...I could use a hand around here. There's a room upstairs you can have for part of your wages if you want it." He paused and thought for a moment. "You ever thought of running a damn little fish market one day, son?"

Kenneth Roberts just stared at the man as tears came to his eyes once more, and then he laid his dinner on top of the banana box, grabbed Raymond's hand in both of his own and began shaking it again vigorously.

"Thank you, sir. Thank you so much."

"I'll take that as a yes," Raymond said, patting Kenneth on the shoulder.

He thought for another moment and then looked Kenneth in the eye. Deciding, he waved the younger man over to the counter, pulled several twenties and a key on a small ring out of the cash register, and handed them to Kenneth.

"Here's an advance and the key to the room upstairs," he said. "Stairs to the entrance are around back. Buy yourself a new set of clothes and some toiletries, get a shower and a good night's sleep, and then come on down at 8:00 to help me open up. Tomorrow's Saturday, so it'll be busy."

"Yes sir, I will indeed," Kenneth said, practically beaming now. "I'm a hard worker, Mr. Anderson, and a quick learner. I'll do a good job for you."

"I've no doubt you will. And call me Ray. Everybody does," he said. "Oh, and buy yourself a fishin' pole, too."

"Well...okay, but I don't know how to fish. Never been fishing in my life."

"But you're a quick learner, right?"

Kenneth laughed, "Yes sir."

"Okay then, it's settled. Fishin' on Sunday, me and you. And you can tell me how in the hell you managed to lose that farm of yours," he added with a wink, and then gave a wave and went to finish stocking his crawfish.

School Work

Pete Wazinski left his third hour Math class and headed for his locker. He had Gym class fourth hour, and this year they made them "dress out," which meant he had to go to his locker and get his shorts. Pete hated Gym. He never was a good runner, and Mr. Conklin made them run ten laps at the beginning of class each day. But as much as he hated running, Pete hated dressing out more.

On the first day of school that year, Benny Smith and Rod Minx stole both his jeans and his gym shorts from off the locker room bench. Pete sat in the locker room practically the whole class period with nothing on but his underwear.

Finally, he found a towel in someone else's locker, wrapped it around himself, and went to sit in Mr. Conklin's office until the period was over. Conklin notified the principal, who dragged Rod and Benny out of their fifth hour classes and back down to the gym. They got a three day suspension for the prank, but would not divulge the whereabouts of Pete's pants.

The principal had to call his mother at work, and she arrived at the school with another pair of jeans and took Pete home for the day. On the way home, his mother had tried to make him feel better by stopping for a sundae at Dairy Queen, but it didn't help much. When he got on the bus the next morning, he found that he had a new nickname: Petie Pants.

On this particular day, as Pete rounded the corner and headed for the section of puke yellow lockers, he was confronted with what had become an increasingly common sight at Knox County Middle School. There was a fight going on in the hall, and this time it was taking place only inches away from Pete's locker. *Great*, he thought, *just my luck, and look who's beating the crap out of some poor wimp today—my old pal, Benny.*

Pete hung back, leaning against the cement block wall, watching the show with the others who had gathered to do the same. He was wishing a teacher or one of the school's principals would come along and break it up so he could get his shorts and get to class before the bell rang. If he was late, Conklin would make him go to the office to get a tardy slip, which meant he'd be in the hall alone. Not a wise move. It also meant that he'd be one tardy slip away from getting kicked out of the

Honor Society. No matter how good your grades were, they allowed students to be tardy only three times.

"You little prick, you took my pen. That's *my* pen. You're gonna give it back, *now*, and you're gonna remember never to take *any* of my stuff again. Got that, pervert?" Benny screamed as he beat the kid's head against Mary Welch's black and white pencil sketch the Art teacher had hung on the wall the day before.

"Here, you can have the pen, but I didn't take it, I swear. My dad bought me this pen at Wal-Mart last night. I'll call him and you can ask him for yourself. Please, Benny, I think my head's bleedin'."

"Shut the hell up, jerk. Your shitface daddy didn't buy you nothin'."

As Pete watched, he became sicker by the minute. Not because he was worried about being late for Gym class anymore, but because he could see his own face in place of the victim's. And he thought the kid was right. He thought he could see a red spot on the grey orangutan's belly in Mary's sketch.

Suddenly, Ms. Johnson burst through the group of students opposite him. *Finally*, he thought, *somebody's going to do something*. Pete liked Ms. Johnson. She was his favorite teacher last year in seventh grade. It wasn't just that she was so pretty and young; it was also because she was so nice. She brought in a stereo CD player on the first day of class and told them they could listen to it while they worked as long as they behaved. Everyone behaved, and she became one of the most popular teachers in the whole school.

"That's enough, Mr. Smith! You and I are taking a walk. If Mr. Haggert doesn't call your parents, I will!"

"No way, bitch. I'm not spending the rest of the day in old man Faggot's office."

"I'm sick of this type of behavior. Let's go. *Now,* Benny, *right now!"* She nearly screamed the last part, and then grabbed hold of Benny's arm.

Pete and the other students watched in horror as Benny turned away from his victim and in one swift move, punched Ms. Johnson in the face. Pete looked just long enough to see that her nose was beginning to bleed before he stepped up to Benny and proceeded to try to beat him to a pulp.

Benny had about fifty pounds of muscle and a good six inches on Pete. It would have been no contest. But luckily, Mr. Haggert broke through the crowd of kids just in time to see Benny's hands lock around Pete's throat. Before Mr. Haggert dragged him off, Benny had time to whisper in Pete's ear.

"Tomorrow. Shop class. You're dead."

The next morning in homeroom, Mrs. Hoit had to call his name a second time before Pete responded with a dry "Here." He hadn't slept at all the night before trying to come up with a plan,

146

some way to handle his little problem with Benny. He had thought about telling his mom, but he was afraid she'd do one of two things, neither of which would help him in his present situation. He thought she would either be really upset that someone had threatened to kill him, or she'd tell him he had to learn how to stand up for himself. If she did the second, it would get him nowhere. And if she did the first, it would probably be very bad.

He could imagine her marching into the school with him, right past the lunch room where everyone had to sit until the bell rang that allowed them to go to homeroom. Some loud mouth would surely see them, and it would be all over the school by first hour that Petie Pants had brought his mommy to school to help him fight bad old Benny Smith. Who knows, she might even make a scene in the principal's office like she did the time Emily "Snotnose" Washington pushed him off the monkey bars in second grade and gave him a concussion. That would just make all the Bennys in the whole school crawl out of the woodwork and come after him. They'd see him as fresh chicken meat for sure.

No, he didn't think telling his mom was the answer. He thought about lying, telling her that he didn't feel well. But he didn't think she would let him stay home by himself if he wasn't feeling good. And she had some important presentation to give for the Board of Directors at the bank, so he didn't want to screw that up for her. Besides, he just hated to lie.

He had also tried to call his two best friends until nine o'clock the night before, but neither was home. His mom didn't allow him to call anyone past nine. He knew Bill had a game and probably wouldn't be home until late. His family usually ate at some fast food joint on the nights Bill had a game. But he couldn't imagine where Sean and his family were when he called and got no answer.

By the time his alarm went off at 5:45 that morning, he'd decided it would be best to just face Benny and get it over with. But before he left for school, Pete did two things. He prayed that there really were such things as guardian angels. Then, he reached in his top nightstand drawer and grabbed the Swiss army knife his dad had given him, just in case the prayer didn't work.

Pete's parents divorced when he was seven, and his dad moved from their home in Charleston to New Mexico. He thought about calling his dad long distance when he couldn't reach Bill or Sean the night before, but he wasn't sure what time it was in New Mexico. He figured with his luck, he'd end up calling at 1:00 a.m. or something. Besides, he thought his dad would just tell him to tell his mother, and that would put him right back where he started.

While Pete sat reflecting on the possibilities he'd decided against the night before, Mrs. Hoit finished calling roll and began answering stupid questions from the chronic won't-pay-attention students. He was suddenly pulled away from his troubled thoughts and back to the moment when everyone in the seats in front of him turned around and stared at the back of the room. When Pete did likewise, he saw a kid just standing by the door with his hands casually stuck in his pockets. He was of average height and weight, but extremely fair skinned with hair so blond that it was actually white. What Pete noticed first, though, were his eyes. *They just don't look right*, he thought.

"Hello, can I help you?" Mrs. Hoit asked when she noticed the kid herself.

"Good morning. I've just transferred to this school. The lady in the office assigned me to your homeroom. My name's Gideon, Gideon Reed."

"Oh! I wasn't aware you were coming, Gideon. Well let's see, you can take that empty seat by the door. Shanda, will you give me a hand and get Gideon one of each textbook please? I think we've issued all of the Social Studies books, Gideon, but Ms. Waters may have one for you. Did they give you your schedule at the office?"

"Yes ma'am."

As Mrs. Hoit rambled on about the class rules, the proper care of text books, and the new student's locker assignment, Pete heard several snickers and a whisper from somewhere to his right.

"Yes ma'am. Oh shit, this kid's gonna get the dissin' of his life. I can't wait."

Pete looked around to see who had said it, but everyone was still staring straight at Gideon. When he turned back toward the new kid himself, he saw that Gideon was staring right at Rod Minx, the creep who had helped Benny steal his pants on the first day of school.

"What the hell are you staring at, asshole?" Rod hissed quietly, but loud enough for Gideon to hear.

Unbelievably, at least to Pete, Gideon just stared at Rod with a goofy smile on his face. The new kid looked, well, peaceful, he thought. Rod, on the other hand, looked disgusted. He shook his head and turned away. The class was stunned that Rod made no further threat.

By the time lunch rolled around, Pete had forgotten about Gideon. He hadn't seen him since homeroom. He hadn't forgotten about his upcoming sixth hour encounter with old Benny Smith, though.

"Do you mind if I sit here?"

Pete looked up to see Gideon standing beside him holding a tray. "No, sure, have a seat. Listen, somebody should have told you that the cafeteria food stinks. Nobody eats it unless they're starving."

"Really? Well, someone should tell the cooks."

"Yeah right." Pete chuckled.

Sitting this close, Pete was now sure of it. The new kid had grey eyes. He'd never seen anyone with grey eyes before. While Pete was thinking of Gideon's strange eyes, Bill and Sean plopped down on the opposite side of the table, already engaged in conversation.

"You gotta quit lettin' those awful dogfarts, Sean dude. You're all worried about how to get Lisa to like you and you sit right next to her letting dogfarts all through the condom film today. You're hopeless, man."

"It was dark; how could she know it was me?"

"She smells with her nose, idiot, just like the rest of us, not her eyes."

"So you guys got to watch Mr. Jones and Ms. Thompson sweat through the condom movie today, huh?" Pete asked. "Pretty funny, wasn't it? Word is they're having an affair."

"Yeah, so we heard," Bill said. "Hey Pete, did you call my house last night? My mom said somebody called about a billion times and just hung up."

"Yeah, I called. Where were you guys? I needed your help with something and neither one of you were home."

"Let me guess. You called because you want us to help you fight Benny in Shop class today, right?" Bill said sarcastically.

Bill was a big kid, and he was a jock, so he got a lot of respect. But he wasn't ever too excited about getting involved in other people's problems, even his best friends'.

"No, I wasn't going to ask you to actually help me beat up on him or anything. I just wanted your brains to help me figure a way out of this."

Pete had forgotten that Gideon was setting across the table. When he suddenly spoke, it startled him and he got choked on his Pepsi. His mom used to put those box drinks that come with their own little straws in his lunch until he told her that the kids made fun of him for drinking baby drinks. So now, she packed a tin foil wrapped Pepsi in his brown paper lunch bag.

"I don't think you'll have any trouble with Benny today, Pete," Gideon said quietly but confidently.

"Oh! Sorry. This is Gideon, you guys. He's new. This is his first day. Gideon, these are my buds, Bill and Sean."

"Hey," the boys said in unison.

"Hello." Gideon smiled.

"You got funny eyes," Sean said, being his usual undiplomatic self.

"So people tell me," was all Gideon said in reply and continued to smile across the table as the bell rang, ending their lunch hour.

Before the boys went their separate ways, Pete's friends slapped him on the back and wished him luck. Bill added that he should tell Mack if Benny started anything funny.

Marshall Mack was the Shop teacher and was considered to be very radical by both the students and the school administration. He allowed kids to make things like bookends in the design of marijuana leaves, and metal sheaths to go around their disposable cigarette lighters. But the one thing Mr. Mack would not tolerate in his classroom was fighting. The kids respected Mack. In turn, the administration respected him and overlooked his unconventional teaching style.

Before he parted company with Bill and Sean, Pete happened to glance toward the door of the cafeteria's kitchen and saw Gideon talking to one of the cooks. *Weird kid*, he thought. Out in the hall, Pete stopped in front of the office. He was about to walk in and tell them that he was sick when he felt a hand on his shoulder.

"Going to Science class, Pete?"

Pete looked over at Gideon's smiling face. "Why are you following me?" he asked.

"You asked me to. Besides, we have the next class together."

"I asked you to? I never asked you to follow me around. And how do you know we have the next class together? I've never seen you even look at your schedule."

"I have a good memory I guess," Gideon replied, still smiling. "Are you angry with me?"

"Well, no, but..."

Pete wanted to question this new kid further. There was something about him that wasn't quite right—something different about him other than his eyes. But instead, Pete simply nodded and walked on with Gideon without saying a word. He didn't have time to wonder about the kid's strangeness at the moment. He still had not come up with a way to deal with Benny during Shop class, which was now only an hour away.

"The Brain," as Mrs. Phiffer was called by the student body, ecstatically announced to the class that they had all passed their last Science test with a grade of "C" or above. She rewarded them with a free class period.

A vote was taken and the majority opted to spend the period outside. With a final word of warning to stay away from the neighboring elementary school kids out for recess, she let the class out the back door. The Science room was one of only a few that had a door leading directly out of the building. Mrs. Phiffer told the class on the first day of school, while stressing the importance of handling the chemicals properly, that this was necessary in case of an emergency, like an explosion.

Pete walked slowly out the emergency door and sat down with his back up against the building. He looked across to the elementary school's playground and wished, just for a second, that he was nine or ten again.

His attention was drawn to a girl on the swings who was yelling insistently. She was asking another girl standing on the ground behind her to stop pushing. She kept telling her that she was going to fall off, but the girl on the ground ignored her pleas. She continued to push on the girl's back each time the motion of the swing sent her backward. Pete watched as the girl on the swing fell off. She landed hard on her back and Pete could tell by the look on her face that the impact had forced all of the air from her lungs.

As she lay on the ground gasping, Pete jumped to his feet and looked around the playground for a teacher. He spotted three of them sitting together on a bench. One was looking in the direction of the swings, but did not attempt to rise from her perch and move in that direction. Pete's face turned crimson and his eyes stung as tears threatened. He made one step in the direction of the swings when he heard Gideon's voice beside him.

"She'll be fine. See?"

Pete looked at Gideon and then back toward the swings. The girl who had fallen was crying, but seemed to be okay. *At least she can breathe now*, he thought.

He watched as she stomped over to where the teachers sat, and in a dramatic tirade that seemed comical to Pete from a distance, began flinging her arms wildly back toward the swings. To Pete's surprise, one of the teachers got up, motioned for the girl's tormentor, and made her sit beside the bench. The girl who had fallen from the swing went off smiling to try her luck on the monkey bars.

"She could really have gotten hurt," Pete said.

"Yes, but not today."

Pete turned back to Gideon, who was smiling, as usual. Then Mrs. Phiffer called the class in, and he felt his stomach roll.

Pete groaned audibly when he entered Shop class and saw that a substitute was sitting at Mr. Mack's desk. He knew that having a substitute would definitely give Benny the advantage. Some of the other students were taking advantage of the situation already. Blocks of wood and small hand tools zipped through the air.

Most of the kids had been in Pete's Science class the hour before, and the free time outside seemed to have set a mood. Having a sub during the last hour of the day was icing on the cake.

Surprisingly, the class period went by relatively uneventfully. And with only ten minutes left before the 3:00 bell, Pete thought that Benny had forgotten all about his threat. He was now actually able to concentrate on the heart shapes he was cutting out of the sides of a foot stool with the jig saw. It was a Mother's Day gift, and he was trying hard to get the hearts perfect.

Suddenly, Rod grabbed Pete's right arm and twisted it behind his back. Startled, Pete jerked to his left and his head connected with Benny's chest. Benny quickly grasped Pete's left hand before he could do anything to stop him and began easing it toward the whirring saw blade. As Rod spit obscenities and threats in his ear, Pete realized that he couldn't reach his pocket for the Swiss army knife. So he said another prayer instead.

"Who you talkin' to, asswipe?" Benny hissed.

Pete began to sweat. He could feel the wind from the saw blade on his finger, and strained to pull it back. He thought of trying some move, maybe stepping on Benny's foot, hard. But he was afraid any sudden move and his finger would connect with the blade--it was so close.

"Excuse me."

"What the hell do you want, you little weird eyed...

"You really don't want to do that."

Pete recognized the voice. It was Gideon. He couldn't believe this new kid was actually trying to stand up to Benny and Rod. *He has to be friggin' nuts*, Pete thought.

Although he couldn't turn around, he knew Gideon was standing directly behind him. And he knew that he was smiling.

Slowly, Benny's grip loosened, and Pete felt Rod's body twitch before he released his right arm. His tormentors grunted a few times, as if trying to speak, but neither said a complete word.

Marshall Mack's substitute came back into the room just as the bell rang, and kids began to scatter, including Benny and Rod. Pete shut the saw off and slowly turned around. Gideon was gone.

Carl McKinney was sitting in homeroom at Elmhurst Junior High in Wyandotte, Michigan a couple of weeks before Memorial Day. He was praying and fighting the fear that was rising in his throat when the teacher announced that a new student would be joining their class for the brief remainder of the school year. Gideon Reed stood up and smiled at everyone.

The Fateful Fruitcake

Paul needed a snack, so he sat the TV remote on the side table, got up with considerable effort, and shuffled off to the fridge. It contained little that was not past the sell by date or free of mold, so he grabbed the fruitcake instead. He hated the holidays—all the traffic, long lines, smiling faces, and fussy kids. He had to admit that the fruitcake was good, though, especially Flo's.

He shuffled back to the sofa in the living room to resume channel surfing and eat his selected supper. His landlady had been giving him a fruitcake for Christmas for going on fifteen years now. *Sweet woman. Still pretty too, despite getting on in years,* he thought. She was always fussing over him. He enjoyed letting her.

Paul had moved into 6B of the Darlington Arms Apartments in Mobile the year before Flo's husband, Jeffrey, took a dive down the apartment's elevator shaft. An unfortunate accident, the coroner had said. Dropped all six floors. Broke his neck on impact.

He changed the channel again, wiped his nose on the sleeve of his robe, and then unfolded the foil from the fruitcake. He sat it on the corner of the littered side table, bent over it and took a big whiff, and then smiled. Flo always put rum in the batter, and it smelled as though she'd given him an extra dose this year.

There was a time he thought of asking her to marry him. But he wised up. *Why buy the cow when you can get the milk for free*, he remembered his dad saying. And besides, he'd done her a favor getting rid of that two-timing husband of hers. *Unfortunate accident.*

He'd been married once himself, back when he was young and stupid. It didn't last long, though. She packed a bag, cleaned out their joint bank account, and then left one day while he was at work. It was on the first day of spring, a week before their second anniversary. She moved back home to Georgia and he returned the gold necklace he'd bought her.

A few months later, her daddy promptly paid for their divorce so his little girl could quickly remarry after she got knocked up by the Macon Baptist minister's son. *Macon bacon*, Paul thought, and laughed out loud.

He broke off a hunk of the fruitcake and crammed it in his mouth. He chewed slowly, his eyes closed, savoring the first bite as the ten o'clock news warned of an extremely resistant flu strain believed to have originated in Denmark, dubbed The Double Danish Flu. *Same shit, different day,* Paul thought.

Feeling a little groggy, he finished off the flat liter of Coke that had been sitting on the side table for a few days and started clicking the remote button again, hoping to find an old war movie. A wave of dizziness hit him but quickly passed. *Probably that damn Double Donuts or whatever,* he thought.

As he flipped through the channels, he chewed another hunk of fruitcake and got choked on it. Coughing violently, he stood up quickly, intending to fetch a glass of tap water from the kitchen, but was violently shoved back down on the sofa by an incredibly strong, invisible force.

Startled, scared and still choking, Paul tried once more to stand but couldn't. He then caught a slight movement out of the corner of his eye and jerked his head around. Sitting there beside him on the sofa was Jeffrey.

Paul looked down at his own chest and saw that Jeffrey's arm was across it, holding him in place. Then he watched, paralyzed, as Jeffrey smiled, reached around him with his other arm, grabbed a hunk of the fruitcake from the side table, and stuffed it in Paul's mouth. He then clamped his widow's former lover's mouth shut.

Superstitions

"No, I'd never been to Brazil before. As a matter of fact, I'd never been out of Alabama except on two occasions: once to Disneyland for my high school senior trip, and once to the Poconos for my honeymoon, which was a waste, by the way, because my marriage only lasted two years.

"I promised myself years ago that before I turned forty, I would visit a foreign country. I thought that if I didn't do it by the time I was forty, I'd soon thereafter lose all desire to travel. I thoroughly believed I'd end up like my mother and find that ultimate pleasure was curling up on the sofa with a glass of iced tea and watching a daytime drama, home decorating, or talk show on TV.

"But to answer your question, Lieutenant, I actually went because Isabella asked me to.

"Yes, she was being sent to Brazil by United Express, the company she worked for, to negotiate the lease or purchase of a building in downtown Belo Horizonte, which I eventually learned means Beautiful Horizon in Portuguese. It was indeed a very beautiful city.

"Isabella said she had visited Brazil before, but for some reason, she was really worried about traveling there alone this time.

"Yes, as I said before, it was very strange, so unlike her. Isabella was used to the world travel that her job demanded. She was so concerned about this particular trip, however, that she actually considered calling in sick.

"I'd known her for years, Lieutenant, and this just wasn't like her. Isabella was no slacker, and I'd never known her to be superstitious. She was a young, vibrant, focused climber—well on her way up the corporate ladder.

"She decided against calling in sick when she realized that they'd probably just postpone the trip. Apparently, the other company rep who knew enough about the deal to go in her place had just broken his leg in a skiing accident.

"Well, I think she said that there was no one else to handle the deal. That's why she decided to ask the V.P. if she could take someone along with her this time. She called me the next day saying that he had agreed to pay for a companion to accompany her, all expenses paid. She asked if I wanted to take advantage of the freebie.

"No, I really wasn't concerned about the strange feeling she said she had about the trip. My mother is superstitious and it has driven me crazy my whole life! Once when I was about twelve, I walked under a ladder, just to be rebellious I guess, and she became nearly hysterical. The next day, I came down with chicken pox, and she kept saying 'I told you so!' But it was just a coincidence. Several of my friends had the childhood illness at the time, so I'm sure I caught it from them…not from walking under a ladder.

"Still, I'll admit that I've never been able to walk under another ladder since then. And I still catch myself starting to say 'bread and butter' if I'm walking with a friend and we go in opposite directions around some obstacle in our path. Mother always says that doing so will 'cut' the friendship, and so will giving someone a knife for a gift. She always says they have to pay you for it, even if it's only a penny.

"I just really don't believe in that stuff, even though a lot of her superstitions did rub off on me. Maybe Isabella had a promotion, I don't know. But I do wish now that she had listened to her instincts and called in sick, even if it would have resulted in only a few days delay. The time difference may have saved her life…and me a lot of nightmares and regrets.

"Oh yes, we'd been there for three days. Sorry, I get sidetracked.

"Yes, we spent the entire time in Belo Horizonte.

"Yes, Isabella came back to our hotel suite with the marijuana on the third day. She said she'd bought it from an American and trusted that it was okay, not laced with anything. She goaded me into sharing a joint with her. She said that since I was throwing caution to the wind one last time before my approaching old age, I might as well enjoy some smoke. Isabella had been teasing me about my female version of a mid-life crisis the entire trip.

"It had been nearly twenty years since I'd smoked pot, so after a second of hesitation, I nodded and she rolled and lit the joint.

"That's correct. Our flight home was the next day. I guess that's why I agreed to smoke the pot with her. I was a little depressed at the thought of going home because I'd been enjoying the trip so much...up to that point.

"The suite at the hotel was just so beautiful. It had a separate bedroom with two double beds, a little kitchenette, and a main sitting area with a comfortable sofa and two arm chairs surrounding a large screen TV.

"I had also enjoyed touring the city. We bought souvenirs, visited so many interesting places, and ate at some wonderful restaurants. I didn't want to leave. So, I thought the pot might boost my spirits before we left the motel for our last night out on the town.

"Yes, we'd found a great little club just down from the hotel and had gone there for a couple drinks each night since we'd arrived. As I've mentioned before, the Comida di Buteco Festival was in full swing, and many of the local pubs were participating. They had each prepared some great appetizers using the same theme ingredient.

"This year, the ingredient they were challenged to use was papaya. Each pub was hoping to win the contest by having the best papaya appetizers. Our plan was to go to our favorite pub again that last night, have a couple of drinks and a bite to eat, and then visit the Parque das Mangabeiras, a beautiful park not far from the city center, just to sit by the huge fountain for a while.

"Yes, that's right. Sorry, I've gotten off track again, haven't I? They started shooting at the door just after Isabella lit the joint.

"No, there was only one door to the hotel room, other than the door to the balcony. I guess we just didn't think quick enough to try to get out that way.

"Looking back on it now, there might have been time for at least one of us to escape. Maybe if we'd grabbed the sheet off of the bed to lower one of us down far enough to jump the rest of the way. I've thought about that a lot, wondering if it would have worked.

"I still can't figure out why they were shooting at the door, though. They couldn't have tried the doorknob first because Isabella didn't lock it when she came in. I'm sure she didn't because of the corny, dramatic way she flung the door open, shut it behind her with her foot, and breezed into the room when she came in with the pot.

"I also can't figure out why they didn't just knock first, unless they assumed two American women wouldn't open the door to just anyone.

"I know it's a strange thing to be dwelling on after all that's happened, but it's an incidental mystery that seems to haunt me.

"Anyway, so yes, they shot at the lock on the door a few times and the doorknob fell off inside the room. When it did, the men barged in. They were two of the most vile looking human beings I'd ever seen.

"As I said, they were both dark skinned, but I have no idea if they were natives of Brazil or not. They were both wearing black slacks and black long sleeved shirts. I think one of them had on a black jacket as well, which was odd because it was so warm outside.

"Yes, they spoke what sounded like Spanish, but it's been a long time since my high school Spanish classes, so I'm not sure.

"The taller man had green eyes and looked a little older than the shorter one...maybe in his thirties. I can't remember as much about the features of the shorter man except for his nose. Something had either happened to it...like it had been burned maybe...or he had skin cancer on it.

Whatever it was, it was horrible to look at. The best way I can describe it is 'decayed.'

"No, Really the only other thing I can remember is that they both smelled bad.

"I don't know, just...bad.

"Okay. Well, things happened very fast after they came bursting in, but my mind sort of goes into slow motion when I recall the details...details I'd just as soon forget, mind you, and probably would if it weren't for the police and reporters constantly questioning me. I think maybe my mind would just block it all out if I didn't have to keep going over it again and again.

"I'm sorry, Lieutenant. I realize you're just doing your job. But I'm tired of remembering.

"Okay. I understand. One more time.

"When they entered the room, the man with the awful nose rushed over to Isabella. She was still sitting at the foot of the bed with the joint in her hand. She opened her mouth and made a strange sound that was probably meant to be a scream. Then he hit her on the forehead with the butt of his gun. I started screaming and the other one reached around from behind me and choked me with his arm until I was unconscious.

"I woke up later...I'm not sure how much later...and we were in a room I can only describe as a dungeon. My throat hurt really bad. The walls of the room were shiny with wetness, and there was a terrible smell of mold and...like oil or something. It was an industrial smell.

"There was only one door, no windows. What little light there was in the room came from a single bulb hanging near the door. I could see Isabella on the opposite side of the room, chained to the wall as I was, but up closer to the door. And I could see her clearly enough to see that something, which I assumed was blood, covered and matted her beautiful long brown hair. We seemed to be alone in the room at that point, and as I came back to my senses, I thought of screaming, hoping someone would hear me, but that thought came too late.

"The men who had attacked us came into the room not long after I woke up. There were three other people with them: a man and two women. They seemed visibly shaken, and I assumed they too were the men's captives. They were Americans...or at least they spoke English and acted like Americans. The man was quite tall, of a fairly medium build, and had sandy blonde hair. He looked to be in his early or mid-forties. The women were both rather short and slim. Both had long brown hair. One of the women had a Boston accent, by the way, in case a missing person's report has been filed on her. I don't think I've mentioned that before. I guess there is a point to going over this again and again after all.

"One of the bad men, shall we say, told the woman with the Boston accent to go over and do something to Isabella. I couldn't hear exactly what, but she protested, looking absolutely crazed.

She kept whining, shaking her head, and repeating 'please no' in sort of a nervous high pitch. After only a few seconds of this, the man with the horrible nose simply shot her between the eyes. The other two Americans screamed. I...I think I wet myself at about that point. But I didn't utter a sound. Not a sound.

"I guess one of the bad men then told the other woman to do the same because she turned and walked slowly over to Isabella, holding both hands over her mouth, perhaps either trying to keep from screaming or from throwing up. Isabella still seemed to be unconscious...or dead. I didn't know which at that point. The woman raised Isabella's dress, and I then understood just what kind of mess we were in.

"The woman began to cry and the good man, the one who was brought in with the women, screamed at her to 'just do it!' As the man screamed at the crying woman, Isabella began to come around a little. I was so relieved that she wasn't dead that I began to cry, but I was very quiet. I didn't want them to know that I was awake and watching.

"The woman seemed to sort of compose herself then. She took a deep breath and stood still for a moment, looking at Isabella. Then she raised Isabella's dress again, gently pushed her legs apart, lowered her head, and began to do what the bad men wanted her to do. Isabella groaned slightly but didn't move.

"I looked over to the men and noticed that the captive man was now on his knees, facing the man with the awful nose, whose back was slightly turned to me. The tall bad man had his gun aimed at the back of the captive American's head. That's when I saw my chance.

"I called to the tall man, who was engrossed in watching both couples' progress, and seductively asked him why he and I should be left out of all the fun. He smiled hideously and walked toward me. I didn't have to ask him to unlock the chains, and as he bent over to do so, I unzipped his pants with my teeth.

"He had laid the gun down to unlock the chains, so I quietly slid it away as far into the dark corner of the room as I could with my foot. While doing this, I pulled at the sides of his unzipped pants with my teeth, exposing his engorged penis, which I toyed with using my tongue.

"He released my right arm quickly, and then my left. Just as he released my left arm, I bit down hard and he immediately doubled over in agony. Before he had a chance to scream, I covered his nose and mouth with my freed hands, jumped on top of him, and began smashing his head into the cement floor with pure adrenalin strength. Soon, his fists stopped beating at me and he laid still.

"I was so afraid his partner had heard and would look over and realize what was going on, but apparently he didn't. The American man was keeping him well occupied. I waited a moment, trying to decide what to do, and then slowly crawled over to Isabella and the woman. Pretending to be interested in joining them,

"I began stroking the American woman's hair. I ran my hands down her shoulders and then around to cradle her breasts. At first, she stiffened at my touch, but then I then pulled her hair to the side, bent as if to kiss her neck, and whispered my plan to her. She nodded slightly, indicating that she understood and agreed.

"We both stood up in front of Isabella then, kissed and fondled each other for a moment, and then slowly walked over to the two men. We suggested by our behavior, that we wanted to form a foursome, which seemed to make the man with the nose very excited. The woman and I began to undress, but then turned to undress the men before taking off much of our clothing. And that's when the man I'd left in the corner screamed out to his partner.

"The man with the nose acted so fast that it's difficult to say for sure exactly what happened next, but I remember he raised his gun, fired, and the woman next to me fell. He fired only once before the American man grabbed his arm. Then, the gun went off again and the bad man fell. We stared at him for a second, not believing he was really dead, I guess. But the bullet had entered under his chin and blown the top of his skull off, so we were pretty sure he was done for.

"I took his gun and cautiously approached the man in the corner. He was either dead now or unconscious again, but I shot him until the gun ran out of bullets just in case. If only I'd made sure he was dead the first time.

"After staring at the man I'd shot for a moment, I sort of came to my senses again. I found the other gun I'd previously shoved into the corner and grabbed it, just in case we needed it while trying to get out of there. At that point, I had no idea where we were.

"I then ran over and checked on Isabella. She wouldn't respond to me calling her name and talking to her, so I shook her, but she just remained limp. I felt her neck and wrist over and over, but I couldn't find a pulse. I put my ear to her chest and listened for a heartbeat, but couldn't hear one.

"I started crying about then, I think. Then I opened her mouth and put my cheek next to it, but couldn't feel her breathing. In a panic, I went over to both of the bad men and searched them for a key to unlock her chains so I could lay her down and try doing CPR, but I couldn't find the key on either of them. I even got down on my hands and knees and searched all around on that nasty floor, but I never could find it.

"Finally, I went over to the American. I told him we had to get out of there...to find someone and tell them what had happened, but he just sat there, holding the woman who had been shot in his arms, rocking her back and forth and staring into space.

"I stayed with him for a few minutes, trying to get him to go with me, but he wouldn't budge. I noticed that she'd been shot in the neck. The bullet must have hit an artery because they were both literally drenched in blood. I assume she was his wife because I noticed then that they were wearing matching wedding rings. I don't think I've mentioned that before either.

"No, I don't have any idea what became of him. I finally gave up and left alone when I couldn't get him to come with me. I just couldn't stand to be in that room any longer, you know?

"I followed along the dark halls, which were lined with lots of pipes and electrical panels and the like. Finally, I came upon an elevator and pushed the button. When the doors opened, I pushed the button for the first floor, unsure of what I'd see when the doors opened again. But when they did, I found myself in the lobby of our hotel.

"I just stood there and stared for a minute, not believing we had been in the basement that whole time. I never got off the elevator. The doors just shut again and I pushed the button for the third floor.

"Yes, our room was on the third floor.

"No, I just went to our suite, nowhere else.

"Yes, I pushed the broken door open, and walked to the balcony. I stood staring out at the city and the beautiful mountains that surrounded it for some time. Not long though, I don't think, but just until I could get control of my nerves. I had started shaking by then, you see.

"Yes, I guess I was in shock. I don't know.

"Anyway, when I finally left the balcony, I got a bottle of water from the fridge and drank the entire thing. Then I went into the bedroom. I showered, dressed, packed, and then got a taxi out in front of the hotel.

"No, I didn't sign out. Isabella had booked the room in her name through the company. I just jumped into the cab and told the river to head for the airport. I only had to wait a couple of hours once I arrived, and then I boarded our originally scheduled return flight home. It was perfect timing.

"No, I didn't inform anyone there of what had happened, and I'm not really sure why. I just wanted to go home.

"Yes, like I said before, that was 6:00 p.m. on the sixth of June. And yes, I did inform the flight attendant when I boarded the plane that the passenger in seat 13B wouldn't be joining us.

Aunt Aggie & Uncle Kit

Aunt Aggie was an unsightly woman. Her perpetual smile and good humor did little to smooth the sagging, weathered skin of her aged face. Thin strands of bronze, straw-like hair stuck out all over her head, which looked about twice as big as a head ought to be, way out of proportion to the rest of her body. She walked stooped over and with an awkward jerking gait, as though one of her legs was shorter than the other. There were no others who looked remotely like her in the hills of Virginia, not even among members of our own family. It was an oddity I don't recall anyone ever pondering aloud.

She was already quite old by the time I was born, and she died when I was a young teenager, but I still remember her vividly. She was a character, an unforgettable one. What she lacked in appearance, she more than made up for in personality. Her infectious laugh and quick wit instantly won you over. And despite her age, she always had a twinkle in her eye, as though she had a grand secret to share.

My mother often enjoyed telling, and retelling, of the days when she was a young girl and would accompany Aunt Aggie on her peddling route. Riding in a buckboard wagon filled with crates of fruits and vegetables, and chickens in cages, they would tour the countryside trading and selling their goods.

One rainy afternoon, a wheel came off of the wagon and its contents went flying, including my mother and Aunt Aggie. The cages broke open and the chickens scattered. Mother immediately jumped up and went running after the chickens, not wanting to lose the day's potential profit. But Aunt Aggie just sat in the mud on the side of the road where she had landed, the hem of her skirt hiked up around her waist, and cackled louder than the hens at their humorous misfortune.

Aunt Aggie was a married woman, if you can believe it. Uncle Kit was about the opposite of his wife in every way. It was surely a strange sight to see the two together, as seldom as that was.

She was about twice as tall and twice as wide as her mate, since Uncle Kit was a small, scrawny man. I never really knew him, had only seen him a few times before he died, but kinfolk always said he was "mean as a snake," and that the older he got, the meaner he got. They say he even killed a man once, just for stealing his milk goat.

So the story goes, Uncle Kit got him with a single bullet from a snub nose 38 Smith & Wesson he carried in the pocket of his bib overalls. The thief made it over 200 yards to the edge of the creek in back of their old barn when, aided by the goat's bleating, Uncle Kit spotted him and aimed true. It was a miraculous feat. He never went to jail for the deed, however. It was in the old days when mountain folk pretty much took care of the law themselves.

Uncle Kit died one summer day just before his 80th birthday. Everyone on the mountain came to his wake and funeral, and reminisced about days gone by. Funerals were very much a social event in those days, no matter how well the deceased was liked, or not liked, by those in the community.

The little white chapel was filled with fresh cut flowers from folks' gardens on the day of his burial. Aunt Aggie played the old church organ with zeal as those in attendance sang "Amazing Grace" and "Just a Closer Walk with Thee."

Picnic tables were set up right on the grounds of the town cemetery, and after the ceremony, everyone enjoyed a fine meal together. There was everything from fried chicken, okra, and green tomatoes to Jell-O salads, sweet tea, and homemade ice cream that were brought in coolers packed with ice.

A few days after Uncle Kit passed away, my mother went to visit Aunt Aggie at their old, dilapidated farmhouse, which was a few miles outside of town. She took her a cured ham from our smokehouse, some green beans she'd canned, and a blueberry cobbler. She said she thought she'd visit a while, but as it turned out, she didn't stay long.

When she drove up the long rutted gravel drive, she got a funny feeling, like someone was watching her. It was so strong that she said she started looking all around when she got out of the car, sure there was someone standing at the edge of the woods or by the creek. But she didn't see a thing, not even a deer or other animal, so she went on into the house.

The feeling didn't go away once she got inside though. Instead, it got worse. She swore that the longer she sat there, the more convinced she became that it was Uncle Kit's ghost watching her. Finally, she just jumped up, gave some crazy excuse for having to leave so suddenly right in the middle of one of Aunt Aggie's famous tall tales, and headed out of there as quickly as she could.

She ran to the car, hopped in, and backed out of the driveway so fast that she knocked over the mailbox that Uncle Kit had made out of an old whiskey barrel. Once she got to the straight, flat stretch of the main highway, the accelerator on her old Chevy didn't leave the floorboard until she reached the edge of town.

That was the last time any of us ever saw Aunt Aggie alive. After hearing my mother's story of her encounter, my grandmother got worried. Aunt Aggie didn't have a phone, and there were no neighbors nearby, so Granny drove out to the old farmhouse to check on her early the next morning.

She found Aunt Aggie lying on the kitchen floor with an egg in her hand. Another egg had rolled out of her hand and landed by her left foot. A pan of water was boiling on the stove.

They hardly ever performed an autopsy back in those days, so no one knows for sure what caused her death, but most assumed it was a heart attack. It was a common demise of the elderly, caused by "hardening of the arteries" or a "weak ticker."

Family members wonder though, if a person really can die of fright. They believed Mom's story about Uncle Kit's ghostly visit, you see, especially since she brought back one piece of physical evidence with her that day. In the side of her old white Chevy, about half way down the rear quarter panel, there was a single bullet hole.

Mr. Jimmy

Marcie was a hairdresser, or Cosmetologist that is. I remember she was always quick to correct you if you called her a hairdresser, or beautician, or anything other than a Cosmetologist. What Marcie really wanted to be was a nurse, though.

All through high school, she worked part-time over at Doc Walker's office, mostly helpin' out at the front desk, but he'd let her help him with patients every now and again. Then, after she graduated, she tried to get into the nurse's college over in Memphis, but she didn't do too good on that test they gave her and they told her to try again the next year.

Well, she did some more studyin', worked at the Rexall Drug Store to learn all she could about medicines and remedies and whatnot, and saved up another twenty-five dollars that it cost to take the test. She tried again but still didn't pass that darn test, so she just gave up and went to Lola's College of Cosmetology in Brighton, the next town over.

Marcie did real good at the beauty college. She passed her final test with flying colors and was real proud. The very day she got her beauty license in the mail, she went to work over at Thelma's Beautyrama. And it wasn't long before she had a slew of regular customers. She'd learned all the latest styles for ladies and men folk alike. Why, I heard tell she was even teaching Thelma some new things. Yessir, she was doing real good, but she didn't get to work as a Cosmetologist for very long. Mr. Jimmy came around that next year.

Mr. Jimmy was a banker. He'd come to town to oversee the setup of the new bank over on Main Street. Why, even back then, right after the war, Mr. Jimmy made real good money. You could tell because he always had expensive store-bought clothes on, even when he wasn't working, and he had a solid gold watch and a ring he wore on his pinky finger. He drove a brand new Dodge automobile to boot! That was the year they had that ram's head with the horns curled up on the front of the hood. Yessir, Mr. Jimmy sure did seem like a real fine feller.

He had all the eligible ladies in town after him, I'll tell ya that much. Why, June and Judy Taylor almost clawed each other's eyes out over him right in front of Bigster's Rexall one Sunday after church. Before Mr. Jimmy came to town, everybody always said there weren't two more lovin' sisters on this whole earth. Most thought there weren't none prettier for that matter. Both of 'em had shiny red hair that came just to their shoulders in little curls, due more to the Toni permanents they gave each other than mother nature, according to their daddy. I remember him talking to Ol' Smitty over at the barber shop one day about what an awful smell they caused. I reckon June and Judy would be mortified if they knew their daddy was tellin' that on them, for I heard them tellin' Bobby Bigster one day that they were buying those Toni permanents for their momma.

Well, like I was sayin', June and Judy both had their eyes set on Mr. Jimmy sure enough until that Sunday in front of the Rexall. But he came walking around the corner and heard the two of them fussin' over him and set 'em straight right then and there.

He told 'em they were two of the prettiest creatures on God's green earth, but would they please excuse him and move out from in front of the door because he had to get into the Rexall to buy some candy, seein' as he was going courting that evening. Why, you should have seen the look on those girls' faces. They sort of stared at him for a second or two, turning red and all, and then just smiled and started walkin' down toward Main Street, arm and arm.

I saw the whole thing, for I was sittin' on the bench outside the Rexall playin' checkers with my nephew Roscoe the day it happened. I reckon that was somewhere around two o'clock, right after church let out, and I'll bet every woman in town was tryin' her best to find out who Mr. Jimmy was courting not fifteen minutes later.

They didn't have long to wait to find out because that evening was Tipton's annual Sadie Hawkins Day dance and Sunday Supper on the Ground. That's why the Rexall was open. Used to, everything in town was closed up tight as a barrel on the Sabbath, but Bobby opened up a couple hours because of all the goings on. Heard he made a fortune that day, too.

Well, like I was sayin', all the women folk figured it had to be the town's big shindig that Mr. Jimmy was takin' his lady friend to. You see, there wasn't much to do for fun in Tipton back then, and Memphis, the closest town with fancy restaurants and a picture show and all, was quite a ways off. So, most everybody was plannin' on goin' to town that evening, and the few that weren't changed their minds just to see firsthand who it was that Mr. Jimmy had taken a shine to. I reckon that's because the whole town had taken a shine to Mr. Jimmy.

Darndest thing was, we didn't really know the feller that well. Most had never even spoke to him. I reckon it was because he was always so happy-go-lucky all the time. Or, it might have been that laugh of his. Why, you couldn't help but cackle yourself when you heard him laugh that way. But I imagine what really got the ladies' hearts to flutterin' was his good looks.

He was a tall fella with a stocky build, sorta like a football player, all muscle. And he had wavy black hair that was longer than most men wore their hair back then. He kept it slicked back, but every so often, a big curl would escape and fall on his forehead. He had a square jaw and a little dimple in his chin, too. And he had them big bright blue eyes. Strange lookin'. Almost unnatural. I heard Thelma Pierce say once that she saw her very own soul in those eyes of his when she bumped into him, supposedly on accident, over at Emma's boarding house one day when she went callin' to drop off a new Avon book.

Anyway, I reckon that's why everybody for miles around turned out for Sadie Hawkins Day that year. Why, there were so many millin' around out at the fairgrounds that somebody stumbled into Chester Jones when he was eyein' all the cakes and pies set around for the cake walk, and he lost his balance and his right elbow went right into the middle of Tammy Sue Jones' pecan pie. Lord have mercy, Tammy Sue was mad as a wet hen at that 'ol boy for the longest. Said she'd been up half the night bakin' that pie from a prize-winnin' recipe out of the *Ladies Home Journal.*

All of us that saw it happen were just about to split a gut laughin' so hard. We knew Chester had been eyein' all of those cakes and pies tryin' to find out which one was Lou Ellen's. He'd told some of us that he'd brought him a five dollar bill to that cake walk, ya see, and was aimin' to make sure no other feller was goin' to buy Lou Ellen's dish and get to walk her home in the dark at the end of the festivities. He was real sweet on her back then.

Well, most were real happy when Mr. Jimmy showed up with Marcie on his arm that evening. Marcie was a sweet little thing, and folks felt kind of sorry for her due to her havin' to practically raise herself and all. Marcie's daddy, that good-for-nothin' George Parsons, ran off and left Marcie and her momma. He just went to pick cotton one day and never came home. Her momma had to work two jobs after that and did the best she could. But some of Marcie's schoolmates made fun of her because she mostly kept to herself and wore hand-me-downs. Hardly anybody had much money back then, but Marcie and her momma were poorer than most.

She sure had herself fixed up real pretty that Sunday, though. She had all that long, blonde hair of hers tied up in big bushy ponytail with a bright pink ribbon. And she had a new pink sundress on that had little black polka dots all over it and a sash that tied in a big bow in the back. Yessir, she was a sight for sore eyes that day. The Mrs. went on and on about how nice she looked.

Marcie made all her own clothes, I reckon, just like most of the other ladies in Tipton. The women folk would go down to Reva's dress shop beside the Rexall and browse through the Sears catalogs. Then, they'd buy 'em some material, use one of their old dresses for a pattern, and make 'em a brand new dress like the one they'd picked out in the catalog. That's all except Stella Woods, of course, who'd never be caught dead in anything but a store-bought dress, according to the Mrs.

Anyway, we saw Marcie and Mr. Jimmy walkin' around town holdin' hands about every day over the next few weeks. They were an item for sure. But it was still a surprise when Marcie's momma told Mrs. Bigster that Marcie was fixin' to marry Mr. Jimmy and move out West with him. That's where his banking company was sending him next, I guess. And this time, they were giving him his own bank to run, so it was a good move for him, I reckon.

He seemed like an awful good catch for a girl who never had much like Marcie. But some said they thought it a might foolish of her to go rushin' into a thing like marriage. I don't reckon anybody got around to sayin' anything to Marcie about rushin' things after they saw the engagement ring he gave her, though. Why, that was the biggest diamond I ever did see!

After she went West with Mr. Jimmy, Marcie was real good about writin' her momma and sendin' some money back home every now and then. But three years passed by and she hadn't been back to visit her momma even once. That's why everybody was so surprised when she showed up back in Tipton last spring. She just pulled up in front of Emma's boarding house in that same 'ol Dodge coup of Mr. Jimmy's one day, but he wasn't with her.

She didn't tell her momma or anybody else that she was comin'. Just showed up. It wasn't that we were so surprised at her comin' back home for a visit, it was those two little red headed young'uns she brought with her that was the thing.

There was a handful of us who spotted her when she pulled up at Emma's that day and headed over to greet her. I ran the Sunoco fillin' station that used to be across the street from Emma's where the new convenient store is now. So, I yelled to my nephew Roscoe to watch the pumps and got over there about the time Emma came out her front door.

Marcie seemed real happy to see everybody. She hugged us all and told us how much she'd missed us, her momma, and Tipton. Then she introduced us to those young'uns, but she never told nothin' but their names at first. A little while later, when we were all sittin' on the porch drinkin' some lemonade Emma made for us, Marcie began to tell who they were. Lookin' back at it now, I figure she waited till the young'uns were playin' out in the yard to tell what she did.

She said the first year that they were out in Texas, everything was just fine. Mr. Jimmy had bought her a nice house and she'd kept herself busy buying furniture and decoratin' and all. But then he came home one day with this woman.

Marcie said she was middle aged and had pretty auburn hair. Said she was dressed real nice, too. Mr. Jimmy told Marcie that this woman worked at the bank with him and had fallen on hard times. He said she didn't have a place to stay, so he told her she could stay with them until she got on her feet.

The lady was real friendly and thankful for their help. Marcie fixed up the guest room for her, and everything was going just fine for about a week. Then this woman, Coralee was her name, as I recall, came home one day with these two young'uns of hers. She told Marcie that they'd been stayin' with a friend, but that the friend couldn't keep 'em anymore.

Well, long story short, Marcie said she ended up babysittin', taking care of them young'uns day and night. Got 'em ready for school, helped 'em with their homework, did their laundry and everything. Their momma and Mr. Jimmy took to comin' home late from work most nights, so they weren't there to help.

About three months passed and Coralee and her young'uns were still living with Marcie and Mr. Jimmy. Marcie said that's when she'd tried to talk to Mr. Jimmy about 'em. Told him it wasn't right for her to be takin' care of this stranger's children, that she had her own chores and things she'd like to be doin'. She asked if the woman had any family who could take them in. He told her Coralee didn't have any family around those parts, and that it shouldn't be long before she had enough money to find her a place of her own.

Well, Marcie kept right on talkin' that day at Miss Emma's without hardly even stoppin' to take a sip of her lemonade. And by the time she finished her story, we all noticed we hadn't drunk much of that lemonade either.

The rest of the story she told is startin' to fade a bit, seein' as 'ol father time has crept up on me some, but I'll try and tell it just the way she told it to us.

Another three months passed and Marcie said she put her foot down with Mr. Jimmy one Saturday when Coralee was out shoppin' and the young'uns were playin' outside. She told him they had to find somewhere else to go. It'd been six months and Coralee should have saved up enough money by then, seein' as she'd been livin' with them and working overtime practically that whole time. She said Mr. Jimmy got real mad then.

He hauled off and hit her so hard that he knocked her off the kitchen chair she was sittin' on, and she landed funny and broke her right arm. She said she was cryin' out in pain it hurt so bad, but he didn't pay her no mind. He told her she would keep right on watchin' those children because they were his, his and Coralee's. Said he bent down over her as she lay there on the floor and nearly spat the words in her face. Marcie said she was so shocked and hurt and heartbroken that she couldn't speak. But that wasn't the worst of it.

She lowered her voice a little and told us that he had his way with her then, right there in the middle of the dining room floor! Said it was downright inhuman, her with a broke arm and all. Said she tried to fight him off, but it was no use. She just laid there and prayed those young'uns wouldn't come in till he was through with her.

But that was the last time he touched her, she said. From then on, he slept in the guest room with Coralee every night. Until they started fussin', that is. Marcie said that whole next week, neither she nor the children got a lick of sleep. Mr. Jimmy and Coralee stayed up pert near all night yellin' and cussin' at each other. Marcie said it was awful, especially with the young'uns hearing it and all.

Well by this time, we were all so caught up in Marcie's story that we were practically holdin' our breath because she hadn't let up in tellin' it since she'd started, but then she just stopped all of a sudden and stared out across the road at the Sunoco station. I remember that real well.

After all she'd told, none of us knew what to say right off. I was about to get my head clear and say somethin' when she spoke up again. All she said though was that Mr. Jimmy had died in his sleep one night. Said he'd come home late, as usual, but that Coralee wasn't with him. When Marcie asked him where she was, she said he laughed and told her Coralee was gone. She'd taken a little vacation, he said, and he doubted she'd be comin' back.

Marcie said he went to wash up then and she fixed him a plate. He ate his warmed up supper, and then went to bed early. Next morning, he didn't come to the table for breakfast, so she went to the guest room and found him dead in the bed. She called the hospital and they came and took him away.

Marcie waited a couple of months after that, but Coralee never came back. Didn't know how on earth to reach her.

Said she was runnin' outa money, so she went to the bank where Mr. Jimmy had worked and asked if she could take some out of their account, but they said he didn't have an account at the bank anymore. Marcie said she was in a panic. She was almost broke and had these two young'uns of his to look out for, plus one of her own on the way. Said she didn't know what else in the world to do but to come on back home.

That's about all there is to tell, I reckon. It's been nearly a year now since Marcie got back to Tipton. She got her a lawyer and sold the house Mr. Jimmy had bought, but there wasn't much left after payin' the real estate agent and lawyer.

Up until last month, she was workin' back over at Thelma's Beautyrama and doin' real good again. She said she didn't think she could do much beauty work because her arm pained her to hold it up in one position too long, but Thelma's husband, John, got her a brand new hydraulic chair so she could raise and lower her customers more and get her arm in a different position every so often.

Marcie still talked a lot about helpin' the sick though, and kept on readin' all those books about medicine and doctorin' like she always did. So, the church took up some money and got her started in nursin' school. She passed that test of theirs with flyin' colors this time.

Stella Woods even pitched in to help and bought Marcie all of her school books, and then bought the young'uns brand new winter coats, if you can imagine that.

That little baby of Mr. Jimmy's that Marcie was carryin' never made it into this world. Marcie went into labor early and it was born dead. We had a funeral for the little thing. Folks pitched in and we got it a little headstone and everything. It was sure pitiful. You know though, Marcie didn't shed a single tear at that baby's funeral.

Not long after Marcie came back home to Tipton, a couple of government men came around. They stayed overnight at Emma's and asked a whole lot of questions around town about Marcie, Mr. Jimmy, and a woman named Coralee.

We didn't tell 'em nothin' though. We didn't know them boys from Adam. And even though they looked right nice and all, looks can be deceivin'.

Other Works by the Author

Vines in the Vineyard:
Poetry for the Seasons of Life

~

The Hanson Collective:
An Anthology of Short Stories by
Contemporary Kentucky Authors

Both available on amazon.com

Coming Soon

16 Coins

Mystery, suspense, and a relentless haunting voice have surrounded Candie Sewall ever since the ghost of Susan Osborn killed her husband and step-son in this YA novel. Only with the help of new friends, a new love, a beautiful but eccentric witch, and 16 coins can Candie silence the voice and vanquish the centuries old curse that plagues her family.

The Keepers of Donner's Bay: Book One

The novel version of the short story "The Keepers" contained in this collection reveals more detail about the adventures of Dr. Celia Mayfield, the seventh Donner's Bay lighthouse keeper, and other residents of the vibrant little fishing village that sits on the banks of the horseshoe-shaped bay.

The Hanson Collective II: An Anthology of Works by Contemporary Kentuckians

This second offering includes short stories, poetry, novel excerpts, creative non-fiction, photography, and artwork by various gifted authors and artists who currently reside in western Kentucky.